# FAITHFUL

*The Mountain Man's Babies*

FRANKIE LOVE

# COPYRIGHT

Edited by Peppermint Editing and Teresa Banschbach

Cover by Mayhem Cover Creations

## ABOUT THE BOOK

### The Mountain Man's Babies

**The moment I saw her I knew.**
**Knew that we would have a future, a family, a forever.**
**Her father says she's too young, too naive, too innocent.**
**But she is more than he knows.**
**She's the love of my goddamn life.**

**She is gone in the blink of an eye.**
**But this mountain was made for miracles, and I'm fighting for ours.**
***I have faith in the impossible.***
**Faith in us.**
**And nothing will stop me from being the man she needs.**

*Dear Reader,*

*FAITHFUL is the epic conclusion to the most romantic series to ever land on your Kindle.*

*I didn't hold back with this one.*

*Suspense. Secrets. Steam.*

*But most of all, babies.*

*I promise you, Jonah is the baby-daddy of the year.*

*Get ready, sweetheart...*

*This trip to Miracle Mountain is gonna be one heck of a ride!*

*xo, frankie*

# PART ONE

*"Where there is hope, there is faith.*

*Where there is faith, miracles happen."*

*—Unknown*

## Chapter One

## JONAH

The walk to the lake is a quiet one. Of course, it is. Some people might think that this no-name mountain town is too small, too old-fashioned — hell, too *fertile* — but I love it all the same.

And after being in Alaska for the last eighteen months, I'm glad to be back home. *Home.* It took a long ass time for me to get comfortable with that word. For years, home was only ever something I wanted to run from. Leave and never look back. Finally, I know where I want to be.

Where I belong.

I've only been back a few days, after I did a

long stint on deep sea crab boats up in Alaska and made a shit ton of cash. Before I came back, I bought a house, sight unseen. Of course, I had my long-time friend Josie scout it out for me; make sure it would be a place I could settle into for a long time.

A month ago, I called her, telling her I need a house. She laughed when I told her I was ready to settle down, just like she had with her husband Beau. "This isn't the same Jonah I remember," she said. "Since when do you want to put down roots?"

"I'm done playing games, I'm over the dating scene. I'm an old man, Josie."

She snorted. "Old? Jonah, you're twenty-six. Not exactly old."

"Not exactly young, either." I sighed, running hand over my beard, wishing I were already back on the mountain I know and love. "And you know I've seen a lot of shit in my day. I'm an old soul, Jos."

"I know, Jonah. And I'd be lying if I said I didn't love this news. Forrest will be so happy to hear that Uncle Jonah is moving home."

Thinking about her oldest son filled my heart with longing. I'd never thought about a family before; hell, every time I tried to find myself a girl on Miracle Mountain it had ended poorly. Josie and I were fast friends — could make one another laugh easily and always had one another's backs. Virginia and I had never been anything more than opposites. I heard she's married now. And Grace and I had tried, but we were too similar; had pasts that were too closely linked. I wanted to run from that shared history, so she and I were never going to happen.

Seems like most people who end up on this piece of Earth find their one true love really fucking fast. Me? I was never lucky like that. So, finally I left for Alaska. Tired of being alone.

Turns out, Alaska is a hell of a lot lonelier than the mountain where all your friends live.

Now, I'm back. With a lakeside cabin, my own dock, my own boat. Not a crab pot in sight.

The weather is gorgeous today: blue sky, not a cloud in sight, and I thank my lucky stars Josie found this place. A private lake nestled in the mountain with no one for miles around.

I'm still learning the lay of the land, and so I set out on a trail I haven't taken yet with a back-pack and lunch, ready to explore. The last owner clearly knew this land like the back of their hand and wove paths throughout the forest to different spots on the small lake.

The wind rustles through the leaves as I walk down the trail, the fresh, clean air filling my lungs as I survey my property. I step over dead logs covered in moss and my feet crunch the pinecones dotting the ground. It's April and the winter snow has finally melted, giving way to wild mushrooms and toadstools, with wild-flowers just beginning to push through the rich soil.

When I get to the water's edge I pause, seeing a woman sitting on a rock slab, all alone. Sunshine is glittering off the waves and it creates a glow around her. Her long strawberry blonde hair is loose, wavy, and thick, down her back, the edges brushing against the rock. She is looking off into the distance, her profile so beautiful, so delicate. She doesn't hear me, and

I don't want to startle her, but damn, I need to get closer.

I walk toward her, drawn to her, and when my foot cracks against a fallen branch, she turns, startled, and lets out a small 'eek'.

Her eyes widen as they meet mine, dark green like the pine trees around us, freckles across her nose and cheeks, and my heart stops. Pounds. Knows.

"Sorry for startling you," I say, stepping toward her, my feet crunching on the fallen leaves. "I'm Jonah Rye."

"Oh, it's okay," she says, her voice breathy, airy. Light. She. Is. Light. "I'm Faith." She bites her bottom lip. "I've just never seen anyone out here. It scared me."

"You come here often?" I ask, walking closer. Willing myself to take it slow. She looks like she scares easily.

She hesitates, then nods, as if unsure if she should answer.

"Not once," I tell her. "I just bought the cabin up the trail."

She closes her eyes, and I notice she has a journal on the rock. A pen in her hand. "I'm sorry. I'm totally trespassing, aren't I?"

"It's okay," I say, close enough to reach out and touch her. "I can share my lake."

"A whole lake for yourself? That's fancy." She smiles, her shoulders relaxing. Good, I don't want to scare her.

I smirk. "Not fancy. Just found a good deal."

"It's beautiful," she says. "I honestly didn't know anyone owned it. Last year after I moved to the state, I was looking at a map of the area, and decided to find every piece of water on these mountains. To explore as much as possible."

"You're not from Idaho?"

She shakes her head. "Nashville. My family moved here last winter."

"And do you like it?"

She smiles. "At first, no. It was so quiet. So lonely. But then spring rolled around, and I was tired of whining. I decided to fall in love."

My eyebrows lift. Love? *Please tell me she's single.*

"And did you?" I ask.

She nods as she takes in a deep breath. "One day I decided to take a notebook and just write everything I was thinking and feeling down. I thought my dad was the writer of the family—he's a songwriter— but it turns out, I'm a writer too. And this mountain is the perfect place to be inspired. Now I feel like they go hand in hand. Words and this place. I'm writing a novel about the sea, and so every day I look for water." She waves her hand in the air. "I'm sorry, you didn't ask for any of that."

I shake my head. "Don't apologize." I'm itching to sit next to her, to keep listening to everything she has to say, I want to know her story. "Mind if I sit?" I ask.

She tucks a strand of hair behind her ear, scooting over. I sit next to her on the rock, looking over my lake. You can't see my place from here, or anything but water and trees; the mountain peaks above us.

"So, it's the mountain you fell in love with, is that right?"

She nods. "Yeah, didn't think it was possible. Always thought I was a city girl. But somehow this place became my home."

"I can relate. Well, not to the city part exactly, but my love affair with this place was a slow burn. It took time. But I just moved back this week and don't plan on leaving."

"Where were you?"

"Alaska, out on crab boat for eighteen months with a bunch of guys."

"Sounds like an adventure," she says wistfully.

"Sounds like prison."

She laughs at that. Her laughter is light and sweet. Pure. "So, are you from here originally, Jonah?"

I shake my head. "Nah, but I have friends here who are like family. Josie and Beau, they live down on the north ridge. And James and Cherish, we go way back. Rosie and I have history too. Do you know any of them?"

Faith nods. "A bit. My father and his wife spend time with them some. But I spend most of my free time up in Eagle Crest. I work at Cup of Joe."

"That town's booming."

Faith shrugs. "Yeah, not like Nashville though."

"You miss it?"

Faith smiles wistfully. "You ever have that feeling, where you know it's time to move on, but you just don't know where you're moving onto yet?"

I give her a wry grin. "Story of my fucking life."

She looks me over, and I know she sees the tattoos that line my forearm. My flannel shirt is rolled up to my elbows, but there are plenty of stories to trace in the ink she can see. I wonder if she could see more than what is on my surface? Most women I've dated never go deeper than that. Maybe I never let them.

"I used to think life made sense," she says. "But along the way, I realized everything is more complicated than I thought. Nothing is black and white. But the gray is kind of terrifying. So much space there, sometimes it feels so big I could get swallowed up whole by a whale."

"A whale?" I undo the top four buttons on my flannel, show her my chest where I have a big grey whale, tattooed.

She reaches out her fingertips to touch it. My skin grows hot as she traces the black lines. "Whales are known for their compassion and solitude, for understanding life and death."

I nod. "Exactly."

"My story," she says, her voice catching. "The one I'm writing, has a working title."

"Oh yeah, what's that?"

"*The Great Whale and his Golden Girl.*"

"Truly?"

She nods, her fingertip still on my skin. I don't want her to pull away. Ever.

For a moment everything stops. The world. The waves on the water. My heart.

She reaches for her journal, flips the pages. Shows me her notes.

The Great Whale and his Golden Girl. Her story.

“Can I show you something?” I ask her, needing more. More. More.

Her.

She nods. “Please,” she says. “Show me everything.”

## Chapter Two

# FAITH

He has eyes that are blue like the water and a smile that could erase anyone's fear. He is confident and looks me in the eyes, and when I traced the whale on his chest, my own heart was pounding. Like it was the first time I've ever come up for air. He's a stranger. But he knows people that I know and so I trust him. More than I should. I follow him, to a place I've never been.

He takes my hand in his and we fit together like a puzzle piece and I don't want him to let go. Maybe ever. I follow him down the trail, toward his cabin, and I want to stay there. With him. A man with a beard and a flannel, whose hands are calloused but whose heart is open.

You can't have a whale tattoo and be cruel. So, when he looks back at me, his eyes bright as the sun, I know I am safe here. With him.

"Ignore the mess," he says. "I want to show you the one thing I brought back from Alaska."

We climb the steps of the porch. It overlooks the lake, and it's beautiful. Different than Dad and Virginia's sprawling farmhouse — this is a quintessential mountain cabin on a lake. Inside there are boxes; furniture that looks brand new. And over the fireplace is a wood-carved orca. I know it's what he wanted to show me.

"Oh, Jonah, it's beautiful." I take in the whale, mounted on a piece of steel so it looks like it is jumping, swimming, moving. The black and white painted details are precise, yet it has a weathered look. Worn. I look at Jonah. Is he tired, too? It sounds like it's been a long time since he's been home.

We stand before the carving, it's nearly two feet high. "I grew up with a family who was really religious," he says. "And in the bible, Jonah makes a lot of mistakes. But he gets another shot. That's kind of my life now, a second chance."

"Did you make a lot of mistakes?" I ask, turning toward him.

He runs a hand through his hair. "I had a lot of baggage. When I left home, I left a lot of people behind, people who could have used my help. And for a long time, shit, I carried that."

I try to understand what he means, but it feels cryptic. "Could you have done anything?" I ask. "For the people you left?"

He lifts his eyebrows. "I was a kid, so no."

"And now you're all grown up. Can you fix what was broken?"

He presses his palm to the back of his neck. "It's fixed on its own. My family was in a cult — it sounds crazy, but it's the truth. And thankfully, the government got everyone who needed saving out, and the other people went to prison. My father included. My mother moved to Arizona, where another following was coming together. I realized she didn't want saving."

"You have no other family?"

"I have a few siblings, grown now, and everyone did like I did — forged a life of their own."

"Whale families stick together," I say. "Live and die, as a close-knit tribe."

Jonah nods. "Yeah, I read they even mourn together. Crazy right? Through thick and thin, the pod sticks together. I never experienced that kind of love."

"My family is like that," I tell Jonah. "My mom died a few years ago. My dad was a wreck, it's why we moved out here. My friends were all going to college, but I couldn't go with them. Wouldn't go. I wanted to be here with my family, wanted to process alongside our little tribe."

Jonah smiles at me. It's a sad smile. Full of longing. Unrealized need. "You're lucky."

I nod. "I know."

"So, your dad, he got remarried then, out here?"

"Yeah, he married a woman named Virginia."

"No shit?" Jonah shakes his head. "I heard she got hitched."

"You know her?"

Jonah nods. "Yeah, she's sweet. Josie says her husband had a bunch of kids."

My cheeks redden. "Yeah, I'm one of them."

Jonah frowns. "Uh, how old are you, Faith?"

"Nineteen." I can see him visibly relax.

"Fuck, you scared me for a second."

"You're not scared anymore?" I ask, teasing him.

He chuckles. "Should I be?"

I shake my head. "I don't bite."

Our eyes meet again. And I swear he looks at me a beat too long. Or maybe it's a beat that is filled with more than any look I've ever been given.

I don't want him to look away.

"How old are *you*?" I ask.

He steps toward me. We face one another. If he kissed me now, I'd melt against him. It's like every exchange we have is deeper than just words. Than just lines. It's like we're sharing pieces of ourselves that no one else will ever have.

"Twenty-six," he tells me.

I smile. "Older and wiser?"

His mouth turns up, dimples appear. I know I am falling. Have fallen. He will catch me. I know he will.

"Only time will tell." He presses his hand to my cheek. Heat rises within me. I step closer. "I want to kiss you, Faith."

"You should," I whisper.

"You're different."

"So, I've been told."

His eyes search mine. "I told myself, when I came back here, I would stop fucking around."

"Good."

His mouth is so close to mine. He smells like a wood stove, smoky and deep. Heavy and warm. I want him to wrap his arms around me and light the fire. I want to burn everything down. Things I've never had before.

"I don't want to hurt you," he says.

"Then don't."

"If I kiss you, it's saying something." His breath is hot against my ear. My body is awake; lit. Alive.

"What is it saying, Jonah?"

"That this is real. You and me."

"You've known me an hour. How real can it be?" I ask but don't believe in my own question.

"Because you can't fake real, Faith."

He's right of course. And when he kisses me it's the realest moment of my life. The words I've been looking for are found and my lips part and his tongue is against mine and everything — *everything* — in this moment is right. The story I thought I'd been writing is all wrong. Because this is the story that makes sense, the one that I want. Everything from before can be ripped up and thrown away.

We'd bring those memories with us, of course, but they aren't the part that will carry us forward. Jonah's hands on my face, his mouth on my mouth — this is where my story begins.

I kiss him, and I sink into a future I can see so clearly with a man I've just met. A man with a whale tattoo and a bruised and broken past. A man walking down a forgotten trail and finding me. Like I was waiting for him.

As he kisses me, brushing back my hair, his hands sure and firm, I give myself over to the mystery of what will come next. I'm not scared. I'm ready.

I'm his.

## Chapter Three

## JONAH

She doesn't just kiss me. She offers me every damn thing she has to give. I feel it, the transfer. The sharing of power, the want.

"God," I whisper in her ear, the heat between us rising, her skin against mine and I need her. All of her. She needs me too.

"This is real," she says, eyes closed, our noses touching, our fingers lacing. Our hearts pounding. This is real.

"You want this?" I ask, needing to hear more than the rhythm of our shallow breath. I need her to tell me yes. This is what I want. You.

Maybe it's because I've been alone for so damn

long. Since my ex, Steph, from Florida. Since way before that. Since forever. I've never ever had a connection like this. Because this — whatever is transferring between Faith and I could only exist in a space where the magic happens.

"I want you," she tells me. I lift her up, her body slightly, her legs wrapping around me. I carry her into my room and lay her down on my bed. Looking her over — this angel. This gift.

Mine.

"Take me, Jonah." She licks her lips, desperation dripping from her words. I understand. My cock rages with desire. For her. Only her. And she pulls off her top, her breasts full, covered in lace. Perfection.

I ease off her jeans, her panties white and her eyes so full of innocence I wonder for a moment if this is wrong. I'm a goddamn man, who knows what it means to fill a woman with myself.

"You're a virgin," I say. She nods. There is no hiding, no pretend. This is real.

"You'll be my first, Jonah Rye."

"And I'll be your last."

Even as I say it, I know how fucking bold the words are, but she doesn't flinch. She takes my words in stride. She nods. "Yes, Jonah, you will."

She knows it and I know it. And it might sound farfetched, this much power to be felt so damn fast, but love isn't a map you can follow; directions aren't given out beforehand. All you can do is follow the trail and hope like hell that the road leads you home.

Faith.

Faith.

Faith. She is my way home. She was at the end of the trail; one I had never walked before. She was waiting for me — hell, maybe she'd been waiting there all along. But today I took the path that led me to her.

I tug off my jeans, toss my shirt aside. She looks me over with her lips parted, her eyes heavy. Her pussy is covered by those panties, and I need them gone. I push them off, unclasping her bra. Her tits are big and round, her cunt so pink and ripe. Everything about her is ready; full of longing.

"You are..." I choke on my fucking words. Her beauty grips me, takes my goddamn breath away. She isn't naive – she is pure. There is a difference. She knows what it means to love and lose and love again. She is no fool, she is strong, and she is vulnerable, and she is asking for what she wants, and I will give it to her. I will give her everything.

I push down my boxers, knowing it's a lot. Our bodies, naked, bare. So much is new, her first everything. And I want her to take all the time she needs.

But she knows what she really needs, and it isn't time. It's me. Against her skin. "Come closer," she whispers, that breathy voice of hers humming with light and hope. So damn ready to give her heart away. I'll keep it fucking safe.

I lean over her, my hand on the base of her neck, and she runs her hands over my length, her eyes closed and her pink tongue licking her lips as she feels me. As she takes my manly length in her hand and feels the weight of that much power.

"Your touch," I moan, my cock aching with desire. Never has a woman's touch felt so damn near perfect. Her gentle stroke a sweet tease, my palm on her round, full breasts — taking her hard nipple between my teeth, sucking, tasting, needing more.

She whimpers, the heat of our bodies is goddamn electric, hot and wild, and she runs her hand over my back, my skin prickling against her touch. I kiss her neck, my hands grazing her bare skin. Her body opens for me, a flower blooming with each touch.

"My body... it's yours," she whispers as my fingers move between her legs, her pussy ripe and tender. "I've never been touched by a man," she tells me. "Teach me what it means to be yours."

God, her words could fucking make me come, here and now, but I want to make this last a long fucking time. All day and all night. I want her pretty cunt to drip, to sing, to learn the rhythm of my body inside of hers.

I will teach her everything she wants to know. And more. I will guide her pussy home, I will take her where she needs to go.

My hand moves against her opening, she is slick and wet, my fingers at her center, her whimpers louder as I circle her clit. I need to taste her, and I ease down Faith, between her legs, my tongue running over her entrance. Her fingers run through my hair, her thighs trembling. I look up. "You okay, golden girl?"

"Yes," she says, her eyes meeting mine. "It's just... I've never felt so many things at once."

My hand stills against her. "Neither have I, Faith." She understands what this means. Not just for her; for her virginity. But for me. "This isn't how it normally goes."

"What do you mean?"

"I just met you, just tasted you, and fuck, I love you."

Her eyes stay locked on mine. "Me too."

It's simple and true and crazy and ours. And when my mouth returns to her cunt, I lavish her with love. It's fucking fast, this rush of emotions, but I don't give a shit. I've spent a long ass time looking, waiting, wanting. Now I found Faith and I won't let go. When you know, you fucking know.

My tongue slides over her, making her squirm with pleasure, and pride swells over me, being her first lover, the only man to ever make her feel this fucking good. She needs more, though; she needs my thick cock inside her, she needs to come hard and fast, to scream my name, to never forget.

Her release is creamy and sweet, and I suck her until she is moaning with need, her clit throbbing. "Oh, Jonah," she pleads as she comes, as she wraps her legs around me, her back arching as my mouth sucks hard against her sweet little pussy.

I move on top of her, her eyes searching mine, her mind rushing into oblivion. I reach for a condom, but she shakes her head. "No. I want to feel everything my first time."

"I'm clean, but you might—"

"I don't care. I'm in charge of my body. Let me decide. And right now, I just want all of you."

I look into her eyes. "You're sure?"

She nods. "I know the risks." She licks her lips. "I want to be a mother."

My eyes widen. "Faith—"

"Do you trust me?"

"You're nineteen, your life is just beginning."

She smiles widely. With confidence and clarity. "Exactly."

I drop the condom, lace my hands with hers. "I will give you anything you want, you understand that?"

"I know you will, Jonah."

"Why do you believe in me?"

"You want to put down roots on this mountain?"

I nod.

She runs her fingertips through my beard. "Then start right now. Start with me."

I could fucking cry— her words are goddamn beautiful, trusting and true, and all I want is to make Faith happy, to help her soar. To spread her wings and be everything she dreamed, and more.

"I don't want to wait to start my story, Jonah,"

she tells me. "Do you want to wait to start yours?"

"I think it started the moment I found you. Everything from before was a goddamn prologue. You are my opening line. The first real sentence. The place the real story begins."

We kiss for a long time, lost in one another; lost in the pages we are only just now finding. We explore each other's mouths, our hands moving as our tongues collide. Moving deeper, touching and teasing until we're nearly blind with want. Until we reach a state of ecstasy that can only be found when you are getting off with a person who truly understands you. I've never fucked like this before — like it meant something so real and deep.

So, when I ease my tip into her wet cunt, I cup her face with my other hand, needing this moment to be memorized. It is ours and no one else's and we will always remember this. How the hell could you forget?

"Take me," she pleads, and I do. I fill her up, slowly, so damn slowly. And I know it hurts at first, she winces as my thick length fills her tight little channel, but I hold her against my chest, the whale tattoo between us. I will protect. I will take of her. I will never, ever let her down.

When my cock is fully in her, she takes a long, shaky breath, clinging to me. "Look at me, Faith."

She does.

"I love you," I tell her, the words foreign and true and new, yet right. "I've never felt this way before."

"Never?"

I shake my head. "Never."

Our bodies move so slowly, so tenderly, with a rush of need that only we can deliver.

"This is love, isn't it?" she asks. Tears in her eyes as we move to a rhythm only we can hear.

"It has to be." I kiss her then, softly, our mouths making promises, our bodies making vows.

Yes. Yes. Please.

## Chapter Four

## FAITH

When he fills me up, the world washes away, and I wouldn't believe I could feel so much, so fast, except I watched it happen with my dad and Virginia. They were strangers who knew the moment they met.

And I know too.

My body thrums to life as his thickness fills me, takes control of me, gives me exactly what I need. His hands run over my bare skin, my breasts, my hips, my thighs. "You're so beautiful," he tells me, and I believe him. I feel beautiful in his arms.

I melt against him, and he rolls me over, so I am

on top of him, looking down at the most handsome man I've ever seen. The scruffy beard and tousled hair, his wry smile that matches his name. His biceps are big, he is strong, he is a man who could possess me in the way I need to be controlled. I've always been a free bird, but he has the power to take me under his wing and keep me safe from the wild world.

I want that. Him. This. Us.

And when I move my hips in a small circle, the feeling overwhelms me. "Oh Jonah, oh my, oh," I moan, the sounds untamed and loud, echoing around us. The sounds coming from me. I press my hands to his chest, and he wraps his big hands around my waist, pulling me to him as we come together, hard.

The sensation so much deeper, so much fuller than my own hand could ever manage as I tried in vain to get myself off. This orgasm is bigger than life and my heart pounds as his hot come fills me.

I want this moment to last forever. Me, in his arms, being filled with his seed.

"Oh Jonah," I cry as his hands run through my

hair, as he pulls my mouth to his, kissing me hard. I don't want him to ever let go.

"Faith," he groans as he finishes inside me. My body warm and full. "God, you're everything."

He holds me close and we try to gather our breath, to gain control, but it feels like everything we had, we just gave one another. We roll to our sides, facing one another.

"Well, that was unexpected," I say, smiling, my skin so hot with pleasure.

Jonah kisses my shoulder. "You surprised me. Being so certain about what you want."

"Life is precious, Jonah."

His jaw tightens, he traces my shoulders, my collarbone, my neck. "You are precious," he tells me.

"You said you loved me. Was that a line or was it true?"

"You really have to ask?"

I shake my head, tears in my eyes. "No."

"Good." Jonah kisses my forehead, his thickness between us, still hard, and my pussy thrums with desire — I need all of him. Again and again. "You said you wanted to be a mother, you mean that?"

I nod. "My mom had six kids. I want a big family, I want to have a legacy."

Jonah smiles. "You're an old soul too."

I pull the sheet over us. "I am. Older than my years, my mom always said."

Jonah's hands run over my body, and I move closer to him. Not wanting any space between us. "So where did you grow up exactly?" I ask, wanting to know everything about him.

"It sounds crazy, but my family was in a religious cult. It was a messy place -- ruined a lot of lives. Tore my family apart. Wouldn't wish it on my worst enemy."

I bite my lip. My own childhood was idyllic-- family dinners and warmth and parents who tucked me in each night. "I'm so sorry," I say, my hands in his hair, tugging him closer. I kiss his lips, softly. Wanting to stay like this with him forever.

"Yeah, fucking heartbreaking, Faith. It's why I

want my life to be about more than suffering. I want to fucking live."

"So, what will you do you do, now that you're back from Alaska?"

He rolls on his back, his head on the pillow. I memorize his profile. His nose, his lips, his long lashes. He groans, looking over at me. "I'm writing a memoir."

My eyebrows pop up. "You're a writer, too?"

"Trying. Not as literary as I'm sure you are, golden girl."

I roll my eyes. "I'm just learning, Jonah. But I want to write something that moves people. Makes them feel something."

He nods. "I get it. I couldn't imagine writing fiction, it seems hard. I love that you are."

"I have a lot to learn," I tell him. "I'm taking some online writing courses; my dad is super supportive. I still live at home, and I work part-time. And I help with the kids. Virginia is pregnant again."

Jonah listens. "I heard that. You like living there?"

"I don't mind. It's practical."

"Are you pretty practical, in general?" he asks. "I need to know these things, considering I've fallen in love with you."

I laugh, incredulous at all of it. I wrap my leg around his thigh, lacing my fingers with his. "I'm practical in nature. But a romantic at heart."

"Which is why you aren't opposed to falling in love at first sight?" He kisses my nose.

"Exactly."

"You know, if you are so practical, you could move in. Would make sense, considering this is a long-term arrangement."

I laugh. "You're crazy."

He nods. "I am."

We lie like that for minutes, staring at one another. And before we blink, before we look away, it doesn't seem so crazy anymore.

"My dad would lose his shit if I told him I was moving in with a man I just met."

Jonah swallows and runs his hands through my

hair. "Is it the older guy part, or the man you just met part that would piss him off the most?"

"It's the losing his oldest daughter part."

"You'd still be on the mountain. A few miles away."

"He'd hate me moving in without being married. He and my mom were pretty old-fashioned."

"They must have married young, considering how old you are."

"They were high school sweethearts."

"So, it's not the age thing, really, is it?" Jonah asks.

"No, it's more of him not knowing you."

"We can change that," he says. "And I'll make an honest woman out of you."

I smirk. "Oh yeah, you want to go meet my dad for the first time and tell him we're getting married?" I laugh. "The look on his face..."

Jonah though turns serious. "That's what I want."

I twist my lips. "What's that?"

"I want to marry you, Faith."

We both go still, the weight of his words between us. I stare at the whale tattoo on his chest. My novel about the great whale and the golden girl, seeming to take place in this small space.

"Alright," I tell him. "I'll marry you, Jonah Rye."

His face breaks out into a smile as wide as the ocean, as bright as the star-filled sky. His arms wrap around me and I know I am his. Now and forever and always. His.

"I think I'll make you a fine wife," I say, rolling on top of him.

He laughs, big and wide and I laugh too. It's crazy and beautiful and I don't care what anyone thinks. This is real.

He lifts my ass, and I sink ever so slowly down on him. "I'm sorry if it hurts."

"It's okay," I whimper, as his arms wrap around me, cradling me. He rolls me over, onto his back. Gently filling me so as not to hurt me.

"My bride."

Tears fill my eyes. "My fiancé."

"When is your birthday?" he asks.

"November first."

"Winter baby."

I nod. "You?"

"April thirtieth."

"Glad we got those details out of the way," I say with a laugh as he moves his body against mine, our skin tingling and hot and alive.

"Coffee or tea?"

"Tea."

He grimaces. "I'm a coffee guy."

"We can work with that," I say, panting as he fills me up.

"Night owl or early bird?" At the same time, we say, 'early bird' and we laugh.

"Books or movies?" I ask.

He brushes back my hair, tucking it behind my

ear. "We're both aspiring writers, how can you even ask such a thing?"

I giggle as his thickness sends a wave of pleasure through me. Between moans, I manage to eke out a reply. "This is insane."

He nods, his cock deep inside me, making me whimper. "Fucking insane."

We come, together, hard. My body revved up and his heart pounding. Both of us gasping for breath as we reach the height, the peak. The climax. God, he fills me up, makes my pussy hum. Makes my body come. Again. Again.

"Oh fuck, Faith," he groans, his thick release inside of me. All of this is new and overwhelming in the most perfect way.

We finish, panting, wrapped up in one another. "I'm going to marry you, Faith."

I look into his eyes. "Yes, Jonah, you are."

"I guess I should introduce myself to your father?" I bite my lip and Jonah senses my worry. "We can wait, tell him later. But damn, Faith, I don't like to pretend."

I nod. "I love that. Your fearlessness, Jonah Rye."

"Also, I need you to move in with me."

"So soon?" I ask, loving the idea.

"Fuck yeah, you're going to be my wife, Faith. We need to get to know one another."

He kisses me then, our laughter and excitement filling the cabin. I savor this, our perfect moment.

I never want to forget. The day I fell in love.

# Chapter Five

## JONAH

We decide to drive separately to her father's place. Faith had parked her car off the road where she found the trail and wanted to get it back.

Before she gets in her car, she kisses me again, and I tell her I'll follow her to the farmhouse, that I have faith that everything will be okay.

"My dad appears rougher than he really is. And Virginia will be there, she helps soften his edges."

I jump in my truck, hoping like hell she's right, knowing that I need to be honest with her father. Even he thinks we're a pair of fools, I can deal with that. What I can't deal with is the idea of not being with Faith.

One afternoon, and I know. She is the one for me.

I follow her down the mountain, the afternoon turning to evening and I look to the horizon as I drive, praying to a God I don't understand for guidance. For direction. For acceptance. If this is supposed to happen, it will. I can fight for what I believe in. I can fight for my love story. And I will.

When we get to the house, I reach for Faith's hand, she looks up at me with eyes filled with hope. She wants this to go well too.

"Virginia and I... when she moved here, people tried to set us up," I tell Faith as we climb the steps. "But nothing ever happened, alright?"

Faith nods. She has an unwavering belief in me. It fucking humbles me, makes me want to be the man she needs.

"When I first moved here, I almost died because I followed a boy to the woods. Virginia saved my life. She is a good woman, and I respect her, so if you had a history with her, I wouldn't blame you." Faith licks her lips. "But I do like knowing you don't."

I run my hand over Faith's cheek, kiss it softly. "I'm going to marry you."

She nods. "I know you are." Her eyebrows dance and she pushes open the front door. "Dad, Ginny?"

Two younger girls bound down the stairs, and they immediately ask Faith who I am.

"It's Jonah," she says. "He's home from Alaska." She doesn't give them any more details, or give them time to ask another question, she just takes my hand and leads me through the house to the kitchen.

The house is loud. Kids argue in the living room as we pass it, there is a baby in a pack n play in the kitchen, and Virginia is standing at the kitchen island, a pregnant belly covered by a red apron, chopping potatoes.

"Hey Fai—" She stops as her jaw drops. "Jon-ah!" She sets down the knife and wraps me in a big hug. "Josie said you were home, but oh my gosh, what are you doing here? This is the best surprise."

A man walks in, tall and built, same as me, a beard and eyes that match Faith's. He takes us in smiling as Virginia introduces us. "Tanner, this is Jonah. Remember Josie talking about her bestie up in Alaska? This is him."

"Good to meet you," Tanner says, offering me his hand. "I've heard good things about you from James. He says the two of you are like brothers."

"Yeah, we go back pretty far."

"What brings you to the house?" Virginia asks, picking up her baby from the portable crib. "You haven't even met Ava. She's a little over a year old."

"She's adorable," I tell her. "I'm so happy for you. It's crazy how this mountain brings people together, isn't it?"

"Speaking of," Faith interjects fearlessly. "Jonah and I need to talk with you both."

Tanner frowns. "Everything okay?"

"More than okay. It's wonderful."

"Wow, okay," Virginia says, setting Ava in a

high chair and offering her a sippy cup, which she promptly throws on the floor. "What's up?"

I run a hand over my neck and look at Faith. She nods, a soft smile on her face. She gives me confidence that surpasses understanding. "Faith and I want to get married, and we wanted to talk to you about it before we —"

"What the hell?" Tanner scoffs, his friendly expression gone. "You want to marry this guy?" he asks Faith.

She nods. "I love him."

Virginia's eyes meet mine and I know she is thinking *what the actual fuck?* but she holds her tongue.

"You just got into town, didn't you? Tanner asks me.

"Yeah, I did."

"We met today," Faith says. "And I know it seems extreme, but we don't actually care. We want to be together."

"She's a child," Tanner says to me.

"No, she isn't," I say. "She's an adult who can make up her own mind."

"She's nineteen, she doesn't know what she wants. And you just met."

"You met Mom when you were young," Faith says. "And you and Virginia were in love after one night. Weren't you?" She shrugs, crossing her arms. "But that's irrelevant. I'm not you."

Virginia takes in a sharp breath. Tanner turns to her. "What was that about?"

"Tanner," she says gently. "Maybe we should sit down and talk."

"I'm not talking about this. Faith, you're too young to get married, not to mention you just met this guy. What, you think you can fall in love after—" His face goes white as his eyes bore into me. "Did you sleep with my little girl?"

Virginia drops her head into her hands and tears fill Faith's eyes.

"Dad, that is so not your business."

"Did you?" he asks me. And I see the anger in his eyes. It's not because he is opposed to love, or opposed to marriage, or opposed to his daughter's happiness. It's because he is protective of the little girl he raised. It makes me respect him all the more. His family is his life, his soul—but that doesn't mean I'm backing down.

"It happened, Tanner. Faith and I, we're knit together in ways we never expected. I'm sorry to hurt you, but it's the truth. I love you daughter and I'm going to marry her."

"Get the hell out of my house," he shouts. Faith is crying, holding on to my arm.

"Daddy, stop it," she begs. "Just listen, believe me."

"You don't understand love, Faith. You haven't seen enough—"

"Enough what, Daddy? Heartbreak? Loss? What? What am I missing?" she cries. "Because from where I'm standing, I've seen enough to know what I want. Enough to know when you find something special you don't let go. You hold on tight."

"You're a child," Tanner tells her again, and Virginia picks up the now crying Ava from the highchair. The poor baby has probably never heard arguing like this.

"What's going on?" Several kids ask, coming into the kitchen. They are Tanner's children. Faith's siblings. I hate for them to meet me like this.

"Would you rather us sneak around and lie? Pretend what we have isn't real until the time is right for you? God, Dad, how stupid would that be? Pretending that Jonah and I aren't in love to make other people comfortable. You raised me to be better than that."

"I raised you to think things through, Faith."

You can feel the anger in Faith's eyes. Her emotions are ragged and raw, and she doesn't back away from them. "I love him." She holds my hand tightly, and I am both in awe and mesmerized. She is magic, this woman of mine. Strength like hers could move mountains.

"I don't care what you call this, Faith, but it isn't changing things. You're not getting married while you're living under my roof."

"Fine," she shouts. "Then I'll move into Jonah's."

Virginia raises her hands. "Kids, go outside and play, please, give us a moment." She hands Ava to the oldest girl. "Tanner, you need to calm down, and Faith, give your father a break, okay?" Then she turns to me. "And dammit, Jonah, you can't fall in love in a day. Are you freaking out of your mind? Do you realize the drama you're causing?"

"How long did it take you to know?" I ask her, knowing enough from Josie to know it was a matter of weeks before she was knocked up with Tanner's baby, a ring on her finger.

"I think you should go," Virginia says. "Go see Josie or something, go calm down. I'll call you when things have settled, okay?"

I look at Faith. Her eyes are so full of anger at her father. I take her hands and lead her to the hallways, her father pacing in the kitchen, unable to meet my eyes.

"I don't want our love story to cause other people pain—" She tries to cut me off, but I continue. "Listen, Faith, your father loves you so damn much. Listen to him without trying to prove your point. He'll come around, he has too. Because I sure as hell am not going anywhere."

"I want you to stay here," she says, her cheek against my chest. I breathe her in, we are far from the ocean, but she smells like salt water and crashing waves.

"I know, golden girl, but your father is about to punch me if I don't leave his property. And I might be cute, but I don't look good with black eyes."

"He wouldn't hit you," she says, pouting.

"He might try."

She sighs, her shoulders falling, and I wrap my arms around her. "Listen, call me when things have calmed down in a few hours. I'm gonna drive over to Beau and Josie's and try and calm down, okay? I'll be with you again before the day is done, I promise you that."

"You'll come back for me?" she asks.

I kiss her softly. "I promise you, I'll be by your side to kiss you goodnight."

## Chapter Six

## FAITH

As Jonah leaves the house, my chest tightens. I want to be in control — I don't want to fight with my dad. I want him to see me as I really am. A woman who knows what she wants.

"Dad," I say, walking back into the kitchen. "I'm sorry for yelling."

He runs a hand over his beard. "I don't know what's gotten into you, Faith. I thought I raised you better than this."

"What do you mean?" I press my lips together, the sting of his words hitting me hard. "You raised a daughter who owns what she wants. Isn't that the hope?"

"My hope was that I'd taught you some sense."

"You and mom got married when you were eighteen."

"It was a different time. And hell, Faith, we had a shit ton of hurdles because of our age. We were poor, and it was hard, and—"

"Happy. You were happy, weren't you?"

Dad looks over at Virginia, tears are in her eyes. I know they must have been talking while I walked Jonah out, and I wish I knew what they'd discussed.

"Happiness isn't everything, Faith."

"I love him, Dad."

"It's been a day," he says, disbelief in his tone. "It's laughable."

"Tanner," Virginia says. "Don't."

"Don't what?" he asks.

"Don't push your daughter away. Faith needs you."

"That man is way too old for her."

"Can't I decide who is right for me and when?"

Virginia wipes the tears from her cheeks, and I step back. Away. Not wanting to be around my father anymore. "I thought you would understand, Dad, after how fast you and mom, and then you and Virginia, fell in love. But it's like you are the only one who gets what they want. Apparently, me having that same happiness doesn't matter to you."

"I didn't say that, Faith," Dad says.

"Then you're okay with me accepting Jonah's proposal?"

Virginia's eyes widen. "He really proposed?"

I nod. "And I said yes. Because I love him."

"You will never marry that fool," Dad says.

My whole body goes numb, my heart falling, falling, falling.

My car keys are still in my pocket. I can't stay here. I need Jonah.

"Don't go like this, Faith," Virginia pleads. But I don't listen. I just push open the front door and run to my car. Clover tries to stop me, asking me where I'm going.

"I love you, sis, I'll call you tomorrow, okay? Don't worry about me," I tell her.

"Love you, Faith," she calls as I shut the car door, as I turn on the ignition, Dad on the porch, his hands fists.

"Love you more, Clover," I say. Then I pull out, and drive to the highway, toward Josie and Beau's place. I need to be with Jonah — he is the only thing that makes sense.

My lights are on, the sky is dark. I try to breathe, focus on the road. I never speed and I won't start now, even though I want to press the gas and accelerate, to leave that fight with my dad in the dust.

Instead, I roll down the window, let the mountain breeze run through my hair.

I may be upset right now, but nothing lasts forever. Dad and I will come to an understanding; we have to. I love him too much to fight with him. When I get to Josie's, I'll send him a text, make sure he knows I am safe, even if I'm not sleeping under his roof tonight.

My shoulders fall and I turn on the radio.

Serendipitously, one of my father's songs comes on the radio.

> And I found her.
> Oh, God, I found her.
> I found her now.
> And I won't let her go.

The lyrics feel like a gut punch. I know Dad wrote this song for Virginia when they fell in love. Tears fall down my cheeks. I know in theory the day has been too much, but in my heart, it feels right.

I'm not some stupid girl who is blinded by sex, by a man's body against my own, by promises that couldn't be kept — no. Jonah is real, my feelings for him are real. And now that I found him, I won't let him go.

As I wipe my face, turning on my blinker, a car comes out of nowhere, barreling down the highway, coming straight at me.

I try to swerve, to get out of the way.

But there isn't time.

In the blink of an eye, my world changes.

I learned a long time ago that life isn't black and white... but it isn't grey either.

A reckless driver, the car coming out of left field, crashes into me.

And all I see is bright white.

## Chapter Seven

## JONAH

When I get to Josie's place, her son Forrest runs out to me, giving my legs a big hug. He's a cutie, and a good big brother to his twin sisters, Lily and Iris.

"Hey there, buddy," I say, swinging him in the air. "You staying out of trouble?"

He gives me a sheepish grin that means he's been giving his mama a run for her money. Beau walks over from the garage and claps my back. "Go tell your mother Jonah's here," he says before offering me a beer.

"I'm good," I say, declining the drink. I want to keep a clear head right now, and most importantly want to be able to drive safely the moment I get word that Faith is ready for me to come to get her.

"Hey Jonah," Josie says from the front door. "Wasn't expecting you."

I climb the steps and give her a hug. "Can you guys talk?" I ask her and Beau. "It's really important."

Josie turns and asks Forrest to go put on a movie for him and his sisters. We walk into the house and Josie tells me to sit at the kitchen table. She's clearly been making dinner, but she ignores it and instead sits across from me, Beau next to her.

"What's going on?" she asks.

I run a hand over my jaw. "I met someone."

Josie's eyes light up. "That's wonderful, isn't it?"

"The thing is, we just met, like, today. And we know. Like, we know we're supposed to be together."

She looks at Beau, and they share a small smile.

There isn't a couple on this mountain that can judge Faith and me for falling so fast.

"We decided to get married."

Beau practically spits out his beer. "Holy shit, that escalated quickly."

I shrug. "It wasn't our plan, but hell, there was no denying that it was real. We're both adults and—"

Josie smiles. "This is insane but like, what on this mountain isn't?" She shakes her head. "Let me guess, it's been a few hours and you already know she's carrying your quadruplets?"

Beau chuckles, and normally, I would too. We've all laughed about the magic that happens on this mountain, but right now, I can't joke around. Not when Faith is so upset. When her father made me leave his house.

Josie speaks up, "Okay, so one: who is this woman, and two: why the long face?"

I exhale. "Do you know Faith? Tanner's daughter?"

They nod slowly. "You and Faith?" Beau lets out a whistle. "Isn't she a little—"

Josie rests a hand on her husband's arm. "Beau, don't."

"She's nineteen, not much younger than most the women were when they came to this mountain," I say. "I understand the concern, I do. But..." I press my fingers to my forehead. "I love her. And I have to be with her."

"I'm guessing her father doesn't agree?" Josie asks. "You decided to get married, went to tell her dad and he got upset?"

"How'd you figure all that?"

Josie smirks. "If you remember correctly, my dad was a little upset about Beau and me."

Beau snorts. "Upset? That's what we're calling it?"

Josie sighs. "He was more than upset. He didn't want me to have anything to do with Beau... and because of it, I spent practically my entire pregnancy with Forrest hidden out in this house. It was awful."

Beau takes a swig from his beer. "As shitty as it was, now that I'm a father, I can see the dad's perspective. If one of my girls ran off with a man I didn't know... hell, it would be hard."

"Maybe I fucked up. I feel awful for putting Faith in a bind with her dad. But hell, we just got excited. And we know how precious life is. Why wait when you know what you want?"

"Your intentions were pure, Jonah," Josie says softly. "But sometimes it's hard for other people to catch up to where our hearts are."

"Shit," I groan, pushing away from the table. "You should have seen how pissed Tanner was."

"He'll come around," Beau says. "Every man on this mountain has nothing but respect for you. You saved my ass with Josie. You put your life on the line helping James find Cherish. You go all in for the people you love, so it's no surprise you did the same thing for Faith."

Josie's phone buzzes on the table, and she reaches for it, reading the text. Her face falls and she covers her mouth. "Oh my god," she whispers.

"What is it?" Beau asks, taking the phone and reading the message for himself. "Oh fuck."

"What happened?"

"Oh, Jonah," Josie cries. "I'm so sorry."

Beau hands me the phone, and the words on the screen pierce my heart; shatter my bones.

It's a group text from Harper to all the woman on the mountain.

> *Horrible car crash on the highway.*
>
> *Tanner's daughter, Faith en route to EC General.*
>
> *Prayers needed.*

The thread is blowing up already, but I can't look. My eyes blur and heart pounds and Josie is gathering me up, directing Beau to keep watch over the kids. She kisses him goodbye, but I can only process one thing: Faith is headed to the hospital.

Josie has me in her car and as we're headed toward Eagle Crest, panic sets in.

"It's okay, Jonah. She's going to be okay."

"What if..."

"Don't. Just wait."

"Harper's text... it's not good, Josie." I run my hands through my hair, a fucking mess.

"We don't know the details, Jonah. Have faith. It's going to be okay. It has to be." Her eyes are on the road, but her cheeks are streaked with tears, too.

We don't speak — can't speak. The truth of this moment is too bleak. When we get to the hospital, we rush into the emergency room, seeing so many of our friends already there.

Tanner's speaking with a doctor, Virginia is at his side. Laila, Virginia's best friend is here with her husband, Colton. Laila's eyes meet mine and I know she knows something... something about Faith and me. She walks over to us, and Josie takes over.

"What's going on? Is she..."?

"She's in surgery. A car crashed right into her," Laila says, her eyes filled with tears. "The driver died on the scene... but Faith ... she's holding on."

My hands drop to my knees, I try to breathe.

It's fucking impossible. Josie's hand is on my back. "It's okay, Jonah, it's gonna be okay. You need to be strong," she tells me, and I know it's true. But fuck.

Faith has to be alive. Has to be alive. She's mine. My heart and fucking soul. And yes, even though we just met, but that doesn't change a goddamn fact. Truth is, I love her, and she loves me.

This can't be how our story ends.

I walk to Tanner, needing to hear from him what is going on. The doctor has left him, and he stands alone with Virginia.

"Don't," he tells me. "Don't push it, don't fucking push it."

"I need to know if she's—"

"She's not. She's not okay, she's on an operating table," he says, choking on his words.

Virginia takes my hand. "Jonah, we just have to wait. All of us just need to calm down and be patient for an update."

"Patient?" The thought rattles me. I need to do something. Take care of her. Why the fuck did

I ever leave her? Why did I drive away without her?

Everyone in the waiting room understands how tense this moment is — but it's not just about Tanner and me, it's about beautiful, perfect Faith fighting for her life.

Hours pass, and we wait, pacing the floor, desperate for an update.

Finally, in the early hours of the morning, one comes.

The doctor enters the waiting room, and Tanner moves toward him. I am at his heels even though I know he wishes I were gone.

"The good news is the surgery was successful. The bone she broke was her left arm, and she has a skull fracture."

"Can I see her?" Tanner asks, desperation in his voice. It's an emotion I understand all too well.

"The other news, and I am so sorry to tell you, is that she is in a coma. It was not medically induced—"

"Coma?" Tanner asks and the blood seems to

drain from my body. A collective gasp echoes through the waiting room.

My heart falls to the floor, my need to see Faith paramount.

I told her, when I left tonight, that I would be by her side to kiss her goodnight. Now I don't know if the woman I love will ever wake up.

## Chapter Eight

## JONAH

Hours pass, and unless Tanner gives me permission to see his daughter, I won't be able to see her. He hasn't spoken to me once.

"Maybe you should go home and get some rest?" Josie says. "You can get your car at my place and—"

"I'm not leaving, Jos. I know you've got to get back to your family, but she is my family now. She is my everything."

Tears fill Josie's eyes. "Oh Jonah," she says, wrapping her arms around me. "I always wanted you to find happiness, after everything you've been through as a kid, and this is just… it's too much."

I squeeze her tightly, thankful for a friend like her in a time like this.

"I knew you wouldn't leave," she says. "So, I called James. He's on his way, okay?"

I wipe my eyes, trying steady myself. "Thanks, Jos. I'll call if …"

"I know." She gives me a final squeeze before leaving the hospital. I walk to the coffee stand and grab an americano, needing to stay awake. Needing to be on alert for when the moment comes that I'm allowed inside her room.

Soon, James arrives, and he gives me a tight hug. "Fuck, brother," he says, shaking his head. "I'm so sorry."

"I don't need sorries. I just need to see her, James."

"I know." James' eyes meet mine. "You really love her?"

"Josie tell you everything?"

"Yeah." James shakes his head. "Guess the

women have been texting all night. You've got the wives all worked up."

"I never meant to fall like this. And I know why Tanner's pissed but—"

"You don't have to explain a thing to me. I know you, Jonah. I know what we went through in Florida, trying to scrape a life together after the shit we'd seen. I know what kind of man you are. You are the real fucking thing. And Tanner will know that soon enough."

"I need to see her, man," I tell him.

"I know." James hands me a backpack. "Cherish told me to bring you some clothes, so I stopped at your place and got you some things so you can clean up. You go change, I'll go talk some sense into Tanner."

"What kind of man am I that I can't solve my problems on my own?"

James' eyebrows lift, and I see they are filled with emotion, with memories. "Fuck that. A real man has friends who will stick up for him. A real man doesn't go through shit alone. A real man has friends who have his back. I'd never have rescued my wife if it weren't for you. I always prayed I'd have a way to repay that debt — but hell, I never wished for it to be something so tragic as this."

I press my fist to my mouth, choking back my emotions. "I have faith that she'll pull through. She has to."

"I know, Jonah. I know."

Down the hall, I find a bathroom and change quickly, wash my face and brush my teeth. Run water through my hair. Try to take long, deep breaths. God, I hope James can talk some sense into Tanner.

I make my way back to the waiting room, I see Virginia walking toward me. "Hey," I say. "You holding up okay?"

She's been here all night, and considering she's pregnant, I'm guessing she's exhausted.

"Laila is on her way back to come to get me. I need to rest and check on the kids."

"I'm so sorry, Virginia."

She twists her lip, fighting tears. "She's so young, has her whole life ahead of her."

I can't talk. If I try, I'll break the fuck down.

"You truly love her, Jonah?"

"With all my heart."

"Tanner's looking for you. James had a few words with him, and you just have to understand. She's his little girl, Jonah. His baby."

I nod. "I know. I'm not angry, I'm just heartbroken."

"He blames himself," she says. "They fought so bad after you left, and she stormed off, angry with him. If she doesn't wake up... that will be the last thing..."

I pull Virginia to me, her tear-stained face against my shoulder. "She will pull through, Gin. She will."

Eventually, Virginia collects herself and tells me she'll see me soon enough after she gets some rest. I head toward the waiting room, where Tanner and James are waiting for me.

"I don't like this," Tanner tells me. "But hell, I don't know what to do. If you think..."

He's crying then, falling apart and I do what I

must. I pull him into a hug, not knowing what will happen next, where we go from here — but knowing that Tanner is fucking terrified and so am I and at least we have that common ground.

He loves her the way only a father can, and I love her the way only a man who holds her heart can. And I'm not going away anytime soon.

"There is no room for anger here, Tanner. The only fighting this hospital has room for is Faith, fighting for her life. I know you hate me right now, but—"

He cuts me off. "I don't hate you, I hate myself. I shouldn't have forced her hand."

"Tanner," James says. "It's gonna be okay. She will come through."

We stand there, the three of us so different, yet standing here we are of the same mind. Yes, different struggles shaped us into the men we are, different heartbreak taught us the meaning of love, but one thing we all share is our collective love for this mountain, for the people on it. For the community we have built here.

This place was named Miracle Mountain for a reason.

It's not too late to find ours.

I leave them, and a nurse escorts me to Faith's room. She is hooked up to IVs and a breathing ventilator, her long wavy hair loose around her shoulders, her eyes closed, the sunlit freckles across the bridge of her nose.

I sit beside her, take her hand in mine. Her skin is cold, but it's soft, and her fingers are so fine, I kiss them. One by one and my tears fall on her knuckles.

"I love you," I tell her, knowing I need to buy a ring to slip on her finger.

She is my heart, my life, my forever. And I need to sit here, by her side, until she awakens.

## Chapter Nine

## JONAH

Three weeks have passed. Three weeks where we keep vigil, day and night, Tanner and me.

We have come to an understanding... we both love Faith, and neither of us will leave her for long.

The first week we trade places, four hours on, four hours off. By week two, he decides to sleep at home, with his wife and children. "You will stay here, though, won't you?"

I nod, adjusting myself on the small couch in her room, pulling out my phone to read more about comas, about patients who come out of them on their own. Most people wake between two and four weeks. God how I pray she is one of those statistics.

But after another week where she lies silent, unmoving, the doctors run more tests, more assessments, and people begin mentioning decisions.

When Faith's primary caregiver, Doctor Martin, calls Tanner into his office to update him on results of the latest lab work, I sit by Faith's side, my chest aching for the information that Tanner is receiving.

"I'm here, Faith, you aren't alone," I whisper, kissing her cheek. I brush her hair, rearrange the bouquets of flowers that have been delivered. I read her the letters and notes our friends on this mountain have sent, wishing her well, full of love and hope.

When Tanner enters the hospital room, with Doctor Martin behind him, I'm immediately on alert. "Is everything okay?" I ask, setting down one of the cards she received today.

Tanner's eyes are rimmed in red, and I see he is near breaking. "Tell him," he says to Martin.

Clearing his throat, Martin addresses me.

"There have been some unexpected developments, Jonah. Ones we think you need to be privy to."

I brace myself for whatever might come next. The reality of Faith's fragile condition pressing against my chest. "Tell me, what is it?"

"After a round of tests and blood work over the last twenty-four hours, we've come to learn that Faith is pregnant."

The room spins as I try to grasp his words. Tanner is shaking and Doctor Martin grips my shoulder. "I understand this is a shock, it is for everyone. The reality is that Faith, while in a coma, is carrying a fetus. And from our understanding, you were her only partner."

Pregnant. Faith is pregnant with my child. Our child.

I move to her. Her delicate condition is the only thing keeping me from cradling her in my arms, holding her close, never letting her go. "Oh, Faith," I cry. "Your dream, you wanted to be a mother and now... now..." I know I'm holding on by a thread; the news is so shocking and overwhelming that I don't trust myself to fall apart here and now. How fucking unfair, how wrong, how broken. Faith deserves to be present for this news, this moment where her life changes forever.

"We will need you to go to the lab for blood work to confirm paternity,' Doctor Martin says. "Once that has been verified, you—"

"I'll go, now." I stand, collecting myself, needing something tangible to do. For Faith. For our baby.

Tanner's shoulder shake. "My little girl, it's unfair," he says. "Goddammit."

Virginia enters the room, and she wraps Tanner in a big hug, the pain visible on everyone's faces.

I leave them alone, knowing it is too horrific to talk about right now. Tanner and I have barely come to terms with one another, and now this.

Josie comes to the hospital after I finish the blood work and we head to the cafeteria to get lunch. I couldn't tell her about the pregnancy over the phone. Now we are sitting with ham sandwiches and colas, and I tell her the news.

"Holy shit, Jonah. You're going to be a father?"

I nod. "Faith's condition hasn't changed except for this. The doctor says there have been cases where women in comas have carried pregnancies to term. Apparently in the UK, a woman was in a car crash when she was only two weeks pregnant, no one knew, but eventually, it became clear. She delivered the baby while unconscious."

"That's incredible. I mean, so sad, but..."

"Possible."

"So, no one is talking about termin—"

I cut her off, the word causing my heart to pound. "Not at all. Our baby is a miracle, Josie."

"I know, of course, I want this baby to be born as much as anyone. I just don't know how it affects Faith."

I nod. "It doesn't change things, except they will up her calories. That's the biggest concern, her staying strong and gaining plenty of weight." I shake my head, not touching my food. I can't bear to eat at a time like this. "And

Tanner won't look at me. With reason. Fuck, I thought we were making progress and now... shit, Jos. What if she doesn't wake up?"

Josie's hand squeezes mine. "One thing at a time. Have courage."

"I do, but it's so fucking hard. One day is all we had. And now..."

"Now you are having a baby. Focus on that. On being a father. Faith and your child need you now more than ever. You can do this Jonah. You can be the man they need."

She's right of course. I can't change the facts right now. Faith is in a coma and we don't know what that might mean long term.

But short term — today — I need to trust that my family will be okay.

"I can do this," I tell Josie. "I can be a better man than my own father was. I can be strong for my family."

"Just because you never had a good example of a man when you were growing up," she says, "doesn't mean you don't have good examples now."

I run a hand over my jaw, thinking of all the men on this mountain. Jax, Buck, Wilder, James, Hawk, Bear, Beau, Colton, and Tanner. Men who put family first over and over again. Before they became fathers, they were making messes of their lives; they didn't have something—*someone*— to fight for.

Love changed them, forged them by fire, each and every man. And now they have legacies. They have futures that are worth fighting for.

And now so do I.

I don't know when or if Faith will wake up, but I can live like she is here, like she is mine. She is the mother of my child either way.

And I love her more than life itself.

"I guess I have some work to do," I tell her. "My house is still in boxes."

"What do you have in mind?"

"I need to make my cabin into a home. A place where Faith and our child can return to."

Josie smiles through her tears. "You know, I have a few friends who won't mind helping."

I brush the tears away. "Fuck, Josie, who would have imagined this?"

"You're asking the wrong person. I've been here long enough to learn that nothing on this mountain makes sense to anyone who doesn't live here. But this little slice of heaven knows something other people don't."

"What's that?" I ask.

"We trust that love will always, always find a way."

"You'll get the girls to help with the cabin?" I ask.

Josie nods. "Of course."

We stand, our food uneaten. "I need to get back to her," I say. "It's been a few hours."

"I understand," Josie says. "And Jonah?"

"Yeah?"

"Congratulations. You're going to be a daddy."

I nod tightly, not trusting myself not to cry. "Yeah, I am, Josie. Who the hell would have guessed?"

She smiles. “Before it was dubbed Miracle Mountain, it was called Fertile Mountain. It got its name for a reason.”

We say goodbye and I head to the hospital room, needing to sit by Faith’s side — trusting that one day she will wake. She will hold her child and she will be my wife.

I have faith that could move mountains.

# PART TWO

Seven months later...

*"Don't give up before the miracle happens."*

*— Fannie Flagg*

*Chapter Ten*

# FAITH

I open my eyes, as a scream escapes my mouth.

More than a scream, a panic, a terror. Complete and utter pain.

My hands press against my belly, it's huge. Wires are attached to me, everywhere and I'm choking on the tube in my throat and I'm blinded by the lights and the people and I close my eyes, scared. Terrified. Cold and hot. The pain is unbearable, twisting me in two and I brace myself, unable to focus on anything, anyone. So many hands and faces and no one I know and *where the hell am I?*

I fall away, to somewhere else, my brain awake

but my body floating. Floating. Alone. I hear a voice as I float. I'm holding someone's hand, running through a forest, mountain air and clear skies and the smell of cedar.

In a bed, hands undressing me. Laughter. Smiles. I can't see a face. His face. He kisses me. Kisses me.

I'm melting, against him, into him. His body rocking against mine and I smile. I'm happy, so happy. The pain is gone, and I am floating, and he is mine. Who is he?

Mine.

"I love you," he tells me, his voice strong, sure. His breath hot in my ear and my words soft and true. "I love you."

He fills me up, my body his, and he takes me to the edge, over and over again and he kisses me hard. He kisses me gently. My body takes him, and it feels right. So damn good. Perfect. A rhythm, a heartbeat. A promise of forever.

*Marry me.*

*Yes.*

*Yes.*

*Marry me.*

*Yes.*

My eyes open, blinding, fluorescent lights. "Faith, can you hear me? Stay with us, you're okay," a man's voice urges. He's in hospital scrubs, a stranger. And his voice is loud, urgent. "You're okay, just breathe."

I scream instead, the pain seizing me, twisting me. Breaking me. They place a mask over my mouth, and I breathe in, deep. I close my eyes. I float away.

This time a voice, reading to me. Letters. Books. Poems. Hands on my hands, fingers laced with mine.

"I built a crib," he tells me. "For our baby," he says. I look for him, but I can't see him. All I see is bright white lights and I reach for him. I see a statue, an orca on a mantle, a protector. I trace a tattoo. A grey whale. He kisses me. Kisses me. I want to see his face.

"I've been writing," he tells me. "The memoir. But the story, Faith, I don't know how it's going to end." Tears. His salty tears are on my arms, he rests his head on the edge of my bed, praying. Whispers all night long. Faith that can move mountains. Faith in us.

I want to reach out and touch him, turn his face so I can see his eyes. See him.

I can't.

I sleep.

When I wake, I'm in a hospital room, this time, the lights are low. The pain is gone. I look down, the belly still there, but different. A nurse turns to me. "Oh, Faith," she gasps. "You're awake." She says it as if it's a miracle.

Me. As if I'm the miracle.

## Chapter Eleven

## JONAH

I run to labor and delivery, desperate. The day came when I wasn't here. After how many months of sitting by her side, holding her hand all night long, she wakes up.

"Tanner," I pant, rushing into the waiting room. "Tell me she's okay."

His face breaks into a smile — the same smile I saw when Virginia gave birth to their twins this September.

"She's okay. I just saw her. The nurses are with her right now. She's in shock, Jonah. It's a lot to absorb."

I nod. I've spent months preparing, imagining this day, the day our baby was born — but it was my deepest prayer that Faith would be out of the coma to behold the miracle herself. And somehow it came true. The labor pain triggered something in her subconscious and she woke up.

But for Faith, this is all so much to process.

"And her words, was she..." Our greatest fear has been that when Faith wakes her brain activity will have changed. So many people never regain full functionality.

Tanner chokes on a sob, pulling me into the first hug he has even given me. "She's perfectly healthy, Jonah. My little girl was all there. Not missing a beat, though panicked over the baby. But it's been hardly any time. Once she sees you," he says, wiping his eyes. "Once she sees you and holds the baby. She'll be okay."

"The baby..." I have been so focused on Faith that I didn't ask about our child.

"Jonah, breathe. It's okay. Everyone's healthy. The baby is in her room, go on, and go meet your family."

I nod, in a state of shock, barely registering that Virginia and their children are here.

"We all peeked in her room for a moment, but we didn't linger, knowing she needs her energy for the baby."

Clover gives me a big hug.

"Can you believe she had the baby on her birthday? November first, isn't that a crazy coincidence?"

Crazy is one way to put it. But I know it is no coincidence. Nothing about Faith and me has been by accident.

All of Faith's siblings and I have grown close over the last few months. Once they realized I wasn't going anywhere, they latched on. I've been fishing on my lake with her brothers, Levi and Cash, and her sisters, Lily, Willa and Clover helped Josie and the other women on the mountain with setting up the nursery.

"She was so happy to see us," Clover says. "But she's gonna be so much happier to see you."

I walk to the hospital room door with nerves. Suddenly my stomach is all twisted, the moment I've imagined for so long, finally here. Faith in my arms again, our baby between us. It's all I've been envisioning. Gratitude swells through me. How goddamn lucky we are, to have our Faith, here again, whole.

I step into the room, and there she is. She's lying in the hospital bed, a swaddled baby in her arms. Our baby. A nurse is with her, helping, and I know from reading up on it that she can't hold the baby on her own after the C-section, especially considering how weak she is after having been in a coma for so long.

Her hair is to one side, her eyes on our child, and serenity on her face. Peace. Thank god, that is exactly what she needs.

I step toward her, tears in my eyes. She lifts her chin, seeing me and I smile, moving closer, my heart surging with pride. I will finally meet my baby after so many months of resting my hand on Faith's belly, watching our child move in her womb, as she grew our little masterpiece.

"Faith," I say, my voice etched with love. Ready to start our next chapter. "Oh, golden girl."

Her brows lift, knit together. Worry between them, a frown on her face as she takes me in. She blinks as if torn, lost. Confused.

“I’m sorry.” She shakes her head, looking straight at me. “Who are you?”

## Chapter Twelve

## FAITH

The man walking toward me is ruggedly handsome, bright blue eyes, dimples. Flannel shirt and blue jeans and I have literally no idea who he is.

"It's me, Jonah," he says. "Your..." His words fall, he moves closer and I reach for the nurse.

"I'm sorry, I don't know who this man is. Can you have him leave?" I shake my head as the man named Jonah wipes his eyes. "I'm really confused."

"It's me. You know me," he says, trying to meet my gaze. "We're getting married."

"Married?" My eyes widen and I pull the baby closer to me. Baby. How in the world am I even holding a baby? I'm a virgin, a teenager. I don't understand anything anyone is saying.

The baby begins to cry. *My baby*. The baby they say I grew for nine months. Nine months where I was in a coma and I can't remember that let alone this man.

*Married*?

"Faith, our baby—"

I cut him off, imploring nurse Lydia to help me. The last hour has been completely overwhelming and now this man is here, saying he is... I can't even. My chest tightens as I try to breathe, to calm down.

The baby keeps crying and this man reaches for her and I push him away. "Don't touch her," I say.

"Her?" he asks, tears filling his eyes. "It's a girl?"

"Get the doctor, please," I tell the nurse, who takes the baby from my arms, setting her in the bassinet.

"Doctor Martin will be here in a moment, Nurse Janelle is here for you," she says to the other woman in the room. “I’m technically the baby’s assigned nurse.” Lydia’s eyes are on Jonah’s and together they leave with the baby.

I turn to Janelle. “Do you know that man?” I ask. “He said his name is Jonah?”

Janelle turns to me, and I see she is in tears too. Everyone around me is crying and I don’t understand. I don’t understand anything.

“Oh, Faith,” she says. “Jonah has been by your side for seven and a half months. Everyone at the hospital knows him.”

“They do?” I press a hand to my forehead, exhausted, as Doctor Martin enters my room.

He asks me to explain the series of events, to describe what just happened, asking Janelle to confirm it.

“I just saw Jonah in the hallway,” Martin says. “He is quite upset.”

“Well, I’m quite upset too. Apparently, I have a baby!”

“And, it appears, some sort of selective amnesia.”

My shoulders fall, my heart too heavy. This can't be happening. This can't be my story. I was supposed to... to... I close my eyes. It's too much.

"It's alright, Faith, this is perfectly normal."

"Normal?" I sob. "Normal to not remember falling in love, getting pregnant, carrying a baby for nine months? Normal to not remember the father of your child?" I'm shaking, heaving, and I'm only slightly aware of the fact that the doctor and nurse are having a conversation about me. I remember my entire family, every detail... yet the most important pieces of my puzzle are entirely blank.

Somehow, I became a mother while I was in a coma, and now this stranger says I'm going to be his wife.

I close my eyes, and whatever medication the nurse gives me works. I fall asleep, but this time I'm not dreaming. I'm living a nightmare.

## Chapter Thirteen

## JONAH

In the nursery of the hospital, I stand with Nurse Lydia. While I need to speak with Doctor Martin, it's more urgent that I meet my daughter.

*Daughter.*

Never in a million years did I imagine it would be under these circumstances. I prayed Faith would be awake to experience this first moment with me, and she is in technical terms... but she's still so far away. She saw me and thought I was a stranger. Am a stranger.

How could she forget me when our time together has been forever etched onto my heart? I try to still my breaking heart, can't have it shatter here — when I am about to hold my little one for the very first time.

Nurse Lydia unswaddles my baby, as I take in every detail of her tiny perfection. I unbutton my flannel shirt, set it aside, and sit down in the rocking chair. Lydia hands me my daughter, and tears fill both our eyes. I'm glad she is here with me, silent support. I'm not sure I could manage this moment alone.

She steps aside, giving us privacy. I look my daughter over, kissing her fair hair, thick and wavy like her mother's. She smells like magic, like home. Her body is so small. She was born six weeks early and is going to need lots of love to get strong, to make sure her lungs are fully developed, to help her become the healthiest version of herself.

But she is alive and breathing.

She is here.

Lydia tells me she is four and a half pounds. Even though she is a tiny wisp of a thing, her heart beats fast. Strong. She is a fighter.

Her tiny fingers curl around mine and I hold her skin to my chest, wanting her to memorize me. Tears fall from my eyes. If Faith doesn't know me, I pray our daughter will.

---

I try again, later. Stepping into Faith's room. Our unnamed daughter lies asleep in the bassinet in the nursery, having around the clock care from a team of nurses and doctors. The Eagle Crest hospital is small, and that is a plus for us, it means better care and more attention. There was a brief discussion of moving baby and mom to Boise State Hospital, but thankfully the decision was made to keep them here.

The moment I come into Faith's room, I see her stiffen, biting her bottom lip. Scared.

Tears fill my eyes and I try to be the man she needs. But fuck, I'm not prepared for this. To lose her right when I got her back.

"Faith," I try, my voice shaky, my words unable to cross the divide. "I thought we could talk."

She shakes her head, her eyes on the bassinet. "I don't know you," she tells me.

"Try to remember, remember me."

She closes her eyes, sighs. "I'm trying. I swear, but... all of this is more than I bargained for. I remember going to the lake, my favorite lake, and I remember looking at the water and writing in my journal and that's it. Then I wake up and—" Her shoulders start shaking, tears splashing down her cheeks. "I'm a mom. And I don't even... I can't do this."

"You can, Faith. You can and you will." I sit next to her bed, praying she can open her heart to me. "When we made love. you said you wanted to be a mother. You said—"

She cuts me off. "I don't believe it. It makes zero sense. That I would sleep with a stranger. If we just met I would never..." She shakes her head, baffled.

How do I explain that what we shared that afternoon was life-altering? How do I explain that when she met me, we both knew?

How could we have been so certain only for it to turn out like this? She is saying that meeting me is her greatest regret.

"It was love at first sight," I tell her.

She wipes her eyes, long lashes catching the

light of the open window. Her daughter was born on her birthday, November first. A miracle.

"You turned twenty while you were asleep," I say. "We celebrated, your whole family was here."

Faith scoffs just as the baby begins to fuss. Her first day of life has been so emotional. I reach for her, needing to hold my little girl. "I don't remember my birthday. I missed out on so much. And now I wake up to a life I never asked for."

She's sobbing now. Shaking. And I press the button to call the nurse. Faith is terrified, freaking out over the fact that an entire life has been thrust on her the moment she woke from the coma. I can't imagine how scary it must be.

Nurse Janelle enters the room and sees the state Faith is in. She quickly calls in Lydia to come to take the baby to the nurse. I'm torn on where to stay — with Faith or the baby.

But Faith answers for me. "Please," she tells me. "Go."

The words pierce my heart — she wants me to

go. She doesn't remember a thing. Doesn't remember me.

"The baby needs you now," Nurse Lydia tells me. And though it kills to leave the woman I love, I realize Lydia is right.

Down the hall, I walk with my hand on the bassinet as it is wheeled back to the nursery. I sit in the rocker, my darling girl once again placed against my chest, and I breathe her in, hold her close, say a prayer. For her. For Faith. For me. Lord, let us see this through.

Hours pass. Then days. Then a week.

Then two.

Then a month.

Most of the time, a mother would be discharged after three days post-C-section, but Faith is not a typical patient. And her mental state has everyone on edge. Daily sessions with a psychiatrist help her process what she has gone through, but she's weak, exhausted after minimal output. Her emotional recovery is a slow and tedious one.

She is also having twice daily physical therapy

as she recovers from spending so many months in a hospital bed.

Added to that, our daughter was a preemie and considering that her mother was in a coma for the entire pregnancy, they want to give her as much care and attention as possible.

I hold my baby day and night. She is my heart, my light, my everything.

Her mother is more distant with each and every passing day.

I name her Ocean. Faith would have wanted that.

But every day Faith is further and further away.

The doctors say she is suffering from posttraumatic stress, but also postpartum depression — she can't handle being around us, she is a wreck, hysterical every time we try.

And the most heartbreaking thing is knowing exactly why.

If she had never met me, this would never have happened.

A reporter comes out to do a story on this

unprecedented situation — a coma, pregnancy, and selective amnesia create a sensational story — and while Tanner holds firm that no tabloids can do a story on us — when asked for an interview, we decide to let them share the miracle of our daughter's birth with the world.

The cover of the issue is of Faith, holding our baby. The headline reads, "Miracles Still Exist."

Do they ever.

I make one comment for the reporter, "I hope, with all my heart, that one day Faith will remember the day that brought our daughter into the world. But we're just grateful mother and child are healthy, whole — and most of all, that they are here."

Faith's spirits lift when the issue is published, but she stares at the cover as if willing the headline to change. As if hoping she can manifest another story.

One without any missing chapters.

At six weeks, I am ready to bring my daughter home. To leave the hospital. And Ocean is ready too.

"It's time to take her home with you, Jonah," the pediatrician tells me, Tanner and Virginia at my side. "Ocean is healthy, thriving, and you both need a routine that isn't the hospital."

It hurts to hear the truth.

Tanner and Virginia wrap one another in hugs. Faith is healthy, whole too — a miracle none of us ever knew if we'd see.

But Faith hasn't come to terms with motherhood, with me. With the life, we decided to create all those months ago.

"Ocean needs her mother," I say, holding my baby against my chest. I understand the concern, though; a sterile hospital is no place for a healthy baby. She needs her home.

"We know. And Faith will be moving back home in the next twenty-four hours. You will schedule visits, and hopefully, with time—"

I cut him off. "That with time she'll want Ocean in her life?" I kiss Ocean's head, wishing we could start over. Hating this for all of us. That Ocean could have the life I've dreamed for her. One where her mother is present.

"I know it isn't ideal, Jonah," the doctor says. "But until seeing you and Ocean no longer triggers her, we need to take caution. The most important thing is everyone being healthy. Being well."

I blink back tears, my face a constant fucking waterfall. It's time to bring my baby girl home. It should be joyous, a day of love and laughter.

Instead, it's nothing but heartbreak.

*Chapter Fourteen*

## FAITH

When I close my eyes, I see light. I see hope. I see a glimmer of a life I might have had. Smiles. Glittering water. Part of me knows there is something between Jonah and me... there is someone in my dreams and maybe it's him.

But when I try to see his face, everything turns gray.

I try to hold Ocean; a name Jonah came up with. And it feels right. When he suggested it to me, referencing my book, *The Great Whale and his Golden Girl*, I realized he truly does know me. He knows the things that matter.

But then he walks into my hospital room,

Ocean in his arms, so sure of this. Of us. And I my head begins to throb. My heart tightens. I hate what I've forgotten, but I can't fake it. I can't pretend to love a man I don't know.

And Jonah is a man. He holds Ocean with arms so strong, so sure. He looks at our daughter with eyes so full of light and love I know he is a good, true man made to be a father. A provider. A man who knows what it means to love deep and wide.

But he is so much more than I know how to handle. I can't remember being intimate with him — anyone — and the idea that I bared my soul to him, a man so masculine and in control makes me feel small and impossibly young. Childlike. How could I have been with someone so courageous when I feel so innocent? So naive.

So damn stupid.

*Why can't I remember?*

I have my journal in my lap, sitting on the couch in my hospital room. Today I am going home, back to Dad's place. And I'm happy to leave the hospital, but I'm also a hormonal wreck. My breasts are constantly full, and I pump my milk so Ocean can have it... but whenever I try to nurse her, I begin to cry, cry until my shoulders shake and the nurse takes Ocean away, bringing her to Jonah who is strong enough to hold her. To feed her. To care for her.

Strong enough for the both of us.

I try to write out my thoughts. That's what the psychiatrist has suggested I do as I attempt to take control of my life. Yes, I had a baby while I was in a coma, but that doesn't mean I can't learn to connect to this new part of myself — this person who is half me, half Jonah. It's hard, and I am being reminded by everyone around me to be patient, to go slow, to trust myself.

Everyone I guess, except Jonah. He doesn't say anything like that; doesn't look at me like Virginia does. She says, "It's okay, sweetie. It's a lot to take in."

He doesn't talk like Dad, who says, "Everyone is rooting for you, be gentle with yourself."

Jonah doesn't talk like the women on the mountain, either. Rosie and Stella, Laila and Grace, who come with flowers and food. Hugs. I know they spend time with Ocean before they come to see me. And they look at me with pity, with bleeding hearts. With encouraging words, they probably found on Pinterest boards. I know it's meant to help — all of it.

But it doesn't.

The only thing that soothes my worried mind, calms my restless soul, is when Jonah walks in the room with Ocean in his arms.

Jonah doesn't say much. But what he does say always makes me cry.

For what we lost. For what he is so certain we will find again.

"I love you, Faith."

"I love you."

"I fucking love you."

His words are the most simple, but they feel so damn true.

And I want to believe him.

That he does love me. That

in the space of a day we met and fell in love and made a person that was knit together in my womb.

"I've been here every day for months, Faith," he tells me. "I won't leave you now."

And when Ocean sleeps in the hospital nursery, the nurses tell me Jonah sleeps right outside my door. They tell me he never leaves. That I am his one true love.

That I am his.

And so, I write in my journal, the one with the notes for my book, *The Great Whale and The Golden Girl*, my prayer.

I know that waking up was a miracle. That growing a healthy baby despite my condition was an answered prayer.

And maybe it's greedy. To want more when I already have been given back my life.

But I need one more thing.

I need to remember what it was like to fall in love.

"It's time to go, sweetie," Dad says, entering the

room with Clover and Willa, Doctor Martin behind them. My sisters take my bags and smile, but I know they are sad for me. For what's too hard for me to accept. That I am a mother.

"Did Ocean leave?" I ask.

Dad nods. "Jonah took her to his place an hour ago. They came and said goodbye, didn't they?"

I nod. "Yeah, I just... I don't know Dad, maybe I'm messing up."

"Messing what up, Faith?" he asks, setting down my bags. Resting his hands on my shoulders. Doctor Martin steps closer, listening to the conversation.

"Maybe I should try harder. I mean, Mom would never have left any of her babies like this. I remember when Clover and Cash were born. She was sick but she... she was by their side day and night and I'm not even... I'm not even going to be in the same house."

Willa takes my hand. "It felt different when you knew her, and Jonah were at the hospital?"

I nod, my chest tightening as I realize that's

what this is about. "Yeah, I mean, I feel really overwhelmed, but... this whole time I knew she was only down the hall. But now... I want her to know me."

"Faith, she knows you," Dad says. "She has your hair, your nose, your smile. She was formed within you, a few miles distance won't change what is in her heart."

I blink back the tears. "Maybe not, but it will change what is in my heart. I need to be closer to her than I am now."

"As a medical professional, everything about this case is unprecedented, Faith. But if you have a strong desire to be closer to your daughter, everyone will support you in that." Doctor Martin and my Dad share a look. "Jonah can bring Ocean to you, to your father's home. And you can care for her there, with your family's help."

My eyes widen, I shake my head. "No. No, Ocean needs Jonah. Her father. He is the one who knows her best, he has to be the one to take care of her."

Dad frowns. "Faith, I don't understand, sweetheart. What is it you want?"

I take a deep breath. I don't understand why I am having this overwhelming urge to be with Jonah and Ocean, but I know deep in my heart I belong with them.

I don't know what it might look like, they are strangers to me.

But they are also my family now.

And I need to find out who they are.

## Chapter Fifteen

## JONAH

Josie, Beau, Cherish, and James are all waiting at the house when I arrive with Ocean. They have balloons tied to the front porch, food waiting on the table, coffee on.

"You didn't have to go to all this trouble," I say, unbuckling Ocean from her car seat, but deep down, I'm so happy to see my friends.

"Jonah, don't be insane. You need all the help you can get," Josie says.

Cherish chimes in: "You're used to around the clock help from the nurses at the hospital. A night alone with a baby can be a little overwhelming."

I chuckle, resting Ocean against my chest. "Says the woman who brought triplets to a shack in the woods on her own."

James wraps an arm around his wife. "That's true, babe. I think you're underestimating Jonah."

Beau shakes his head. "No man on this mountain underestimates Jonah. You've fucking taken it to the proving grounds."

I exhale, looking around my place, and accept the cup of coffee that Cherish hands me. "You guys seriously made this place amazing."

No more boxes or bachelor furnishings.

"Well, Stella's a pro. She had a vision," Josie says with a smile. "We were just her heavy lifters."

I carry the bag from the hospital into the nursery , taking in the details, seeing the house in a new light now that Ocean is here. The walls are washed in a soft grey, a chandelier that sparkles with seashells. The sheets on the crib have tiny mermaids printed on them, the rocking chair is upholstered in sea-foam green, the pillow resting on it reading, *Dream Big, Little Mermaid.*

"Everything looks okay?" Josie asks, catching me in the nursery alone.

"It looks great," I tell her. "I can never thank you enough."

"Stop it," she says. "So, how did it go saying goodbye to Faith today?"

"Question of the hour, right?" I groan. "I don't know what's going on in her head. She is so sad, Josie. I don't think it's Ocean and me; I think it's this longing for memories she can't find, for the months she lost. Maybe it's wishful thinking, the idea that it isn't us that makes her upset... but God, I hope that's the truth."

"When will she see Ocean?" Josie's eyes are knit with concern, and I understand why. Everyone on this mountain is praying for a light switch to flip inside Faith, for her to want to be with Ocean. It's scary, the idea that she may not connect with her own flesh and blood.

"I'll take her to Tanner's tomorrow. The doctor suggested we try that twice a day, for however long Faith can manage. Hopefully, eventually, it can be for longer." I want to say that hopefully, it will be forever. That Faith will crawl out of the dark place she is in; that she can have the life she was made for. One of happiness, joy, and beauty.

"Someone's pulling up," Beau calls from the living room. The cabin is small, two bedrooms and an open kitchen and living room, so it's easy to hear everything. I step out of the nursery with Josie, Ocean in my arms, hearing tires against the gravel.

"It's Tanner's truck," Cherish says, her eyes meeting mine.

My heart stills, praying that there isn't more bad news waiting for me. I run my hand over my daughter's head, knowing her first weeks on this mountain haven't been easy. The last thing we need is another crisis.

Beau opens the door, the December frost heavy in the air, and I reach for a blanket, covering my little one. Needing to keep her warm. Safe.

In Tanner's truck sits Faith. Her eyes meet mine through the window. *See me,* I beg silently. *Remember us,* I pray.

Tanner walks inside, closes the door. Alone. Faith doesn't leave the truck.

"Everything okay?" I ask.

Tanner nods. "Faith says she wants to stay here, with you and Ocean."

Josie and Cherish gasp. This is good news, and we all know it.

"Why didn't she come in with you?"

Tanner runs a hand over his beard. "She's pretty nervous. About you accepting her, about taking care of Ocean. She needs a lot of help, Jonah. You know that."

I nod, I've been seeing a therapist every week since Faith entered the coma, and I have processed at length the extra help Faith needs right now. I have learned all about PTSD, postpartum depression, and how Faith is struggling to cope. She isn't in danger of hurting herself, or anyone — her doctors are confident in that. The main goal for her is that she gains confidence in her new role as a mother.

"If she comes here," Tanner says, "I just..." He pauses, sighing. "Well for one, do you want her here, and two, do you think you can do this? Take care of both Faith and Ocean?"

I stand there, thinking what he is saying through, grateful that Tanner and I have come to accept our relationship, and that we need one another in ways we never anticipated. At first, I saw him as this dominating patriarch, but I've learned this love for his family runs as deep as the roots of the trees that cover this mountain.

"Tanner, Faith coming here, being here with me and Ocean, it's all I want."

Josie steps forward. "Cherish and I can come and help out, be another set of hands. I know Virginia is busy with your little guy."

Tanner nods. "I'd appreciate that. I get worried. She's my little girl."

I rest my hand on Tanner's shoulder. "She's safe with me, sir."

Tanner chokes back tears, pulling me into a hug. "I know, son, I know she is."

To others, the exchange might have seemed unimportant, but everyone in this room knows how much Tanner's words mean. When I step back, James' eyes meet mine and now he gets it. We lost our families when we left the church where we were raised — lost so damn much. To have the father of the woman I love believe in me? It means the goddamn world.

"We're gonna scoot out," Josie says, Beau at her heels, Cherish and James behind them. "The kids are with a sitter and we need to get back. But call us, Jonah, if you need anything. Anything at all."

"And Harper set up a food tree, so you'll be set for the next month, three meals a day."

I smile. "God, does that woman ever sleep?"

They chuckle as they leave through the front door. Ocean is stirring in my arms. I wonder if Faith will want to hold her when she comes inside.

"If it's good with you, then, I'm gonna let Faith come in on her own, let the three of you get settled without the old man around."

"You're not in the way, Tanner. Stay as long as you want."

"I know I'm welcome, but I have a family at home who needs me. Your family is here, Jonah." He leans over, kissing Ocean's head before heading outside. I watch him through the open door, speaking with Faith who has climbed out of the truck. Tanner sets her suitcase on the ground, and she reaches for an oversized tote bag. From the looks of it, they made a stop at the farmhouse before coming here.

She hugs her father, then waves goodbye. He drives off and she picks up her bags and walks toward me. She's in black leggings and Ugg boots, a black winter parka with fur on the edge of the hood. There is a bite in the December air, and I want her to come inside.

Her long strawberry blonde hair hangs around her shoulders, she doesn't have on a stitch of makeup. Her eyes are wide, taking everything in. The timber on the roofline, the forest surrounding the cabin, the icy lake in the distance. What does she see when she looks it over? Does she remember any of it?

I know what I think when I look at her. I know that she is home.

Chapter Sixteen

# FAITH

When I stand before the cabin, looking at Jonah and Ocean in the doorway, waiting for me, my heart pounds. I want to remember, to know them. But my mind is blank.

A part of me hoped that maybe when I got here everything would click into place, that memories would rush back to me and I could be in the same place as Jonah, waiting, with arms outstretched. His heart is wide open, waiting for me.

But I don't have a magical *aha* moment. Instead, I have that familiar sense of longing. Wishing for memories I don't have.

I grab my suitcase and carry it up the two front steps, walking into Jonah's place.

"Faith," he says. "God, I'm so happy to see you." As if on cue, Ocean starts crying. "I think she's ready for a bottle."

I nod, stepping into his house, and shutting the door. I set down my bag and take off my winter coat. "Sorry, where's the coat closet?"

He pulls open a door, revealing a small and tidy space.

"Sorry," I say hanging it. "I should have known that, shouldn't I have?"

"No," he answers with a grin. "I'm telling you when we fell for one another it was hard and fast. You didn't memorize my floor plan that day."

"No?"

He shakes his head as I hang up my coat, next to his Carhartt coat, his heavy wool jacket. The closet smells like leather and sandalwood. It smells like a man. I blink slowly. Jonah's presence is such a force to be reckoned with. Being here, alone with him, I wonder how I was ever brave enough, confident enough, to give him my heart so quickly.

"You okay?" he asks, his hand on the small of my back. Ocean still fussing in his arm.

"I'm alright," I say, even though I feel pinpricks of pleasure on my skin. Jonah is so patient, so kind — so handsome and intimidating. It's hard to imagine me taking off my clothes for him, our bodies joined as one... he seems so much older and wiser, so capable.

"You hungry? Can I get you something to drink?" he asks, walking to the kitchen. He opens the fridge and grabs a bottle for Ocean.

"No, I'm not hungry," I say, even though it's dinnertime.

"While I feed her, you're free to put your things in the bedroom."

"Actually," I say, looking around his home. My shoulders relax as I take in his space. His home. "Can I try and nurse her?"

He lifts his eyebrows. "You sure?"

I nod. "Yeah, I want... I want her to know me, Jonah."

Relief washes over him. "That's so good to hear, Faith."

I bite my lip. "And I want to know you, too."

He swallows, his eyes dropping to mine. I see a swell of emotion in them, want and hope and longing.

He longs for me.

What he thought we might become.

What we promised we would be — married.

"The nursery is right in here," he says, walking across the room. I follow him into a bedroom that is an oasis, the colors and lighting soft and lush. "It's beautiful," I say, my fingers running over the wall.

"Stella, Buck's wife, she's is a designer. She planned all this out."

I nod. "I met her, and she came to the hospital to visit once. I didn't realize they had done so much here." I look at the dresser, pulling open the drawer. It's filled with pink baby clothes. I can't help but blink back tears. The closet door is open, and rows of dresses are hung, baby gear and baskets with diapers all ready for use. “Wow,” I say, awestruck.

“What is it?” he asks as I sit I the rocking chair, a mermaid pillow at my back.

He offers me Ocean, and I unbutton my blouse, unhook my nursing bra. Jonah turns. “I’ll go,” he says.

“Please, stay.”

He swallows, his jaw tight, back straight. This is all so much for him. But he does as I ask, and sits on the floor, his back against the crib.

I nudge Ocean to my nipple, assuming she won’t be interested. I’ve attempted this only a handful of times and it has always ended with me in a puddle of tears, overwhelmed with the responsibility. But she takes it without a fuss, latching on, looking up at me.

The milk flows freely, and she suckles, kicking her feet until she begins to relax, and as she does, I relax too. Leaning back in the rocker, holding my baby. This time, I’m not crying.

“I really appreciate what everyone did for you, for Ocean — for us. But...” I shake my head.

"Seeing this room set up for her, everything complete — it just reminds me of how much I missed out on. What I lost. It isn't fair."

I run the back of my hand over Ocean's cheek, gratitude sweeping within me that for once I'm not crying as I hold her.

"I'm sorry, Faith." Jonah exhales. "I didn't think of it like that. Everyone was just so excited to help, to get ready for Ocean. It was like... a concrete thing in the midst of so much uncertainty."

"That makes sense," I admit. "How did they know she was a girl?" ask, looking around at the purple and pink accents. "You said her gender was a surprise."

"I wanted to name the baby Ocean regardless, and Stella and Cherish figured most of the room could be blue, green and white either way." Jonah twists his lips. "I'm not a designer, I just wrote the checks."

"Thank you," I say. "Thank you for all of this. My tears feel bratty. Selfish. You're the one..." I squeeze my eyes shut. "You're the one who has been through hell and back."

Jonah moves toward me, kneeling before the rocker. Ocean is sleeping now, milk drool on the side of her mouth, her eyes closed, gentle coos sending a wave of pleasure over me.

"You can cry, Faith. But please know that it's okay. It was an honor to sit by your side all those months, to read Ocean books while she was growing inside you, to tell you stories about growing up, to hold your hand and press my palm to your belly when Ocean would kick."

"You truly love me, don't you?" I ask, knowing the truth. No man would do so much for someone he just met unless it was genuine love, deep, real. Forever.

"I do," he tells me. Tears run down his face. "Dammit, Faith, I miss you. And my heart breaks for you, you did miss out on so damn much. Things that you deserved to experience alongside me. You slept through all those firsts, and the firsts that we shared, you can't even remember. It kills me when I think of it. But Faith, you didn't die. You are here now. Every day, from this day forward is a memory you can hold on to."

I pull Ocean to my heart, kissing her head.

Wishing I hadn't spiraled so hard when she was born, but desperate to give myself grace for the rollercoaster I've been on.

"I want to be strong, like my own mother always was," I tell Jonah. "I want to be here for my daughter — I don't want any regrets."

Jonah wraps his arms around Ocean and me, his beard bristling against my cheek, his strong arms holding me tight, our daughter nestled between us.

"No regrets, Faith. From here on out, you can be the woman you want to be. Strong and courageous. Like a whale."

I inhale, breathing this man in. This man who loves me.

I can be what my daughter needs. And maybe I can be what Jonah needs, too.

## Chapter Seventeen

# JONAH

JONAH

With my arms wrapped around her, Ocean between us, my heart pounds with hope. I want Faith to be strong, healthy, herself — and I feel like her coming here was the right decision.

Of course, selfishly I want her here. In my bed, in my arms, against me forever — but beyond the physical cravings, I have for her, on an emotional level my deepest desire is for her to embrace the life that has unfolded for her, even if she feels resentful over not having had a choice in the matter.

I move back, tenderly taking Ocean from

Faith's arms and carrying her to the crib. With her eyes closed, I put her down without any stirring. I look back at Faith who is buttoning her blouse. The curve of her breast draws my eye, but I look up, into her eyes. Desiring more than she offers isn't right — and if I am to ever win her heart, I believe it will be a slow process. Starting with trust.

"You're so good with her," Faith says, standing from the chair.

"She makes it easy. She sleeps like a champ, takes a bottle super well. We're lucky."

She nods slowly looking me over as if seeing me for the first time. "Yeah," she says softly. "We are."

For a moment I imagine this is when things change; the moment I can finally turn to Faith and pull her into my arms and kiss her.

God knows I've imagined this moment plenty of times.

Dreamt about it.

I want to take Faith against me once more, want her body pressed against mine as I fill her, consume her. I close my eyes, steadying myself. I can't let my mind run away like this.

"You said you were a writer, right?" she asks out of nowhere.

I nod. "Just like you."

She smirks, rolling her eyes. "Trying."

"Isn't that what we're all doing, Faith? Trying?"

"Can I read something you wrote?" she asks, the question surprising me.

"Uh, yeah, sure."

"Really?"

I nod. "Sure, maybe tomorrow I can pull something up for you?"

"Are you busy now or something?" she asks with a teasing smile.

"No, I just..." I look back at the crib. Ocean is sleeping peacefully. "My computer is in my room if you want to come with me."

She walks with me into my bedroom and I look over the room, imagining it from her point of view.

"Is this where... where we..."

I grab my laptop and turn back to Faith. Her eyes are a darker green than I've ever seen them. "Yeah," I tell her. I step closer. "We were outside on the trail, by the lake and then we came inside, and we made love. Right here."

She swallows, licking her lips. "And I was just... I was ready?"

I nod, tucking a loose strand of hair behind her ear. "You were more than ready," I tell her, remembering her pink cunt, so slick, so needy. "You told me it was your first time, and you said —" I shake my head, not wanting to push things with her before it's time.

"What did I say?" she asks, her words breathless, airy. Like the first time we met.

My jaw tightens as I remember the moment. "You said 'you'll be my first, Jonah Rye.' And I told you, I..." I lock eyes with Faith, my hand on her cheek. "I told you that I would be your last."

She whimpers the tiniest moan. Her eyes closed, her breath bated. "And what did I say to that?"

I smile, looking at the most beautiful woman in the whole fucking world. "You said, yes, Jonah, you will."

She shakes her head, pink rising on her cheeks, her eyes brighter now. Hopeful. "I was so bold with you."

I keep my hand on her perfect cheek, dreaming of the moment when she will be ready for me to make her mine all over again. "You can't fake real, Faith."

Her eyes glitter, dance. "I suppose you can't."

I step away, not trusting myself to stand so close without drawing my mouth to hers. Dragging her into my bed. Taking her, heart, mind, soul.

Her eyes fall to my laptop. "Can you show me what you've written?"

I nod, and together we sit down, on the edge of my bed. When I turn on my computer the home screen shows a photo of Faith holding Ocean, cradling her. It's black and white and Faith looks so strong, resilient — slightly overwhelmed, but in that moment, you can see that she is humbled by the beauty in her arms. Ocean looks so tiny, so perfect — so much ours.

"Oh," Faith startles, looking up at me, tears in her eyes. "Jonah it's so ..."

"Beautiful," I say, filling the space. "Fucking beautiful."

She trembles as she watches me pull up a document.

"Maybe this is too much, Faith. Maybe you'd like a rest?"

She shakes her head. "Let me read." She takes the computer from my lap, and together, we read my account of the day Ocean was born.

November 1st

The first time I held her in my arms I knew that I was forever changed. She was so tiny, so perfectly formed, the most unlikely gift I'd ever received. Her mother was down the hall, but I carried Faith's love with me as my daughter was placed against my chest. Her heart beat against my heart; together they would beat for Faith.

Until Faith came back, until she could see once more — that we were for her, not against her. That we were the

beginning of a new story. Until she

could see that we needed her in this

chapter. Until she realized that,

without her, it would never be

complete.

The three of us were a circle, and we needed

her to be whole.

Faith wipes a tear from her eye. "Jonah," she whispers. "Even if I can't remember... I know this is where I need to be. I want to complete the circle."

I close the computer, looking into her eyes, tears filling mine the same as hers. "Welcome home, Faith," I tell her.

I kiss her then, because her chin lifts, her eyes on mine, the desire between us growing, real. Deep.

Her lips are soft, and the kiss is tender. Raw and ragged like the first time all over again.

I love her. So damn much. Now and for always and when I kiss her, I know those words hang in the air. I know she knows and that is more than enough.

Her mouth parts, our tongues collide. The heat growing, real, here.

I kiss her like we have forever, there is no rush. We have time. Not in the way I thought before, where we moved fast, fast, faster still. Tighter. Needing to take hold as if there was no time to lose.

Now I know better.

Now I see time differently. Now I know the true meaning of precious moments. They are to be savored. Memorized.

I cling to them because I understand now what it means to have no regrets. It isn't rushing things — it is holding them tight.

Never letting them go.

It is long kisses, fingers laced, it is tears shed as mouths part. It is treasuring each and every touch as if it might be the last.

It is love, that is what this is.

I could keep kissing her like this as if there was

no tomorrow, but from the other room, Ocean calls for us.

We pull back, our eyes lock, the wave of emotion overwhelming us both.

Salty tears. The tide comes and it goes.

We stand, moving toward Ocean as she wakes.

I have faith in us, I always have.

I always will.

## Chapter Eighteen

## FAITH

After we feed, change, rock, cuddle and kiss our daughter, Jonah carries her back to the crib, where she sleeps. I can't stop smiling, my heart is beating so fast. I want this to all work out so badly.

In the kitchen, Jonah warms up some of the chicken pot pie that Cherish brought for us.

"Smells good," I say, sitting on the barstool at the kitchen island, trying to be present. Truth is, my mind and body are focused on one thing. The way it felt to have his lips against mine.

Jonah's blue eyes fall on mine. He wears an easy smile; nothing about him feels forced. "Cherish is a good cook, and it sounds like

Harper has people delivering food every day for the next month." Jonah grins, his eyes are bright. "I hate to cook, so it sounds like a good plan to me."

I smile, taking the plate of food. Jonah sits beside me, and I feel the electricity between us growing. The kiss in the bedroom changed me, the words he wrote melted me.

I may not remember falling in love, but I understand now why I did so hard, so fast.

Jonah is like none other.

He is mine.

"I like to cook, actually," I tell him. "Growing up with so many siblings, I always helped around the kitchen. But I can imagine not having that on our plate for the next few weeks will be a blessing. I think we're in for a rude awakening without any nurses here to help."

Jonah nods, taking a bite of food. He looks so handsome, even when he's eating. I can't help but wonder if there is anything, he doesn't look good doing. "We've been lucky. But Ocean is only waking three times a night now, she sleeps like a champ."

We eat mostly in silence. I can tell Jonah is wrestling with something, his eyes are dark and heavy. I'm guessing he hasn't had a good night sleep in a long while.

"You tired?" I ask when we finish.

"Yeah, it's been a long—" He stops, shakes his head.

"A long nine months?"

He nods. "Yeah." He takes my hand, squeezing it. "I know you don't remember me, Faith, but I want you to know that I will always be here to support you, however, you need. And I'm so glad you're here. That you're home. The kiss... well it was fucking perfect, but I don't want you to think that is what I am after – you wanting to be here, with our daughter, that is what I have been hoping for."

I twist my lips; his warm hand feels so good against mine. I want to crawl in his bed with him trailing after me. I want to give myself to him the same way I did all those months ago. I want him to be mine, in the way I realize I am already his.

But Ocean begins to cry from the nursery and Jonah and I both start at the same time.

"Go," he says. "I bet she'll quiet right down in your arms."

"You sure?" I ask, not wanting to step on his toes or take over — after all, he has been her rock for the first six weeks of her life.

"I'm sure. I'll just go shower, actually. If that's alright?"

Jonah leaves for the bathroom and I go to the nursery, reaching for my daughter. I offer her my breast, and as she latches on again, I exhale, glad to be avoiding the breast pump for the moment.

"Hey, little one," I say, kissing her head, breathing her in. My daughter.

My little miracle.

After she eats, I change her diaper and put her in a fresh set of pajamas, swaddling her snugly. Then I set her into the crib once more. She is fast asleep, and I tiptoe from the room, keeping the door open so I can hear any noise.

I hear the shower still running and I decide to

clean up dinner while I wait for Jonah. It only takes a few minutes to wash the two plates and forks by hand. Finished, I turn off the overhead lights, switching on a few lamps instead. Then I walk around the living room, taking in his cabin.

When I reach the mantel, I gasp, pressing a hand to my mouth.

I remember this. The orca sculpture.

I narrow my eyes as a memory fills my mind. So clearly, I have to grab ahold of the mantel to steady myself.

*"Whale families stick together," I say. "Live and die, as a close-knit tribe."*

*Jonah nods. "Yeah, I read they even mourn together. Crazy right? Through thick and thin, the pod sticks together. I've never experienced that kind of love."*

I hear a noise behind me. I turn, Jonah is there, in a towel, his hair wet. I choke on the memories as they swirl around me. I move toward him, my knees buckling — taking in the whale tattoo on his chest, I see myself tracing it with my fingertip at the water's edge.

*I reach out my fingertips to touch it. I trace the black lines. "Whales are known for their compassion and solitude, for understanding life and death."*

*Jonah nod. "Exactly."*

*"My story," I say, my voice catching. "The one I'm writing has a working title."*

*"Oh yeah, what's that?"*

*"The Great Whale and his Golden Girl."*

*"Truly?"*

*I nod, my fingertip still on his skin. I don't want to pull away. Ever.*

*For a moment everything stops. The world. The waves on the water. My heart.*

*I reach for my journal, flip the pages. Show him my notes.*

*The Great Whale and his Golden Girl. My story.*

*"Can I show you something?" he asks me.*

*I need more. More. More.*

*Him.*

*I nod. "Please," I say. "Show me everything."*

"Faith," Jonah says now, reaching out to me as I grip the mantel2

o. He pulls me to him.

I look into his eyes. His eyes. Eyes that are as blue as the water. Eyes that could calm the storm.

"You remember?" he asks.

I nod, seeing it. Seeing it all. Seeing him all over again for the very first time.

In his bed, wrapped around one another. No second-guessing. No doubt. A life with him so crystal clear.

*"I want to marry you, Faith."*

*We both go still, the weight of his words between us. I stare at the whale tattoo on his chest. My novel about the great whale and the golden girl, seeming to take place in this small space.*

*"Alright," I tell him. "I'll marry you, Jonah Rye."*

*His face breaks out into a smile as wide as the ocean, as bright as the star-filled sky. His arms wrap around me and I know I am his. Now and forever and always. His.*

*"I think I'll make you a fine wife," I say, rolling on top of him.*

*He laughs, big and wide and I laugh too. It's crazy and beautiful and I don't care what anyone thinks. This is real.*

"I remember." And I do. "I remember everything."

He kisses me, knowing my words are true. You can't fake real. He pulls me to him, his mouth crashes against mine, and I feel the weight of our forever. It is light. Bright. Ours.

"Take me all over again," I ask between kisses. "Make me yours once more."

"I'll make you mine, forever, Faith."

"I love you, Jonah Rye," I whisper. Jonah never wavered in his love, his devotion.

He takes my hand, leads me to the bedroom. Ocean is sound asleep, and I'm grateful because right now I need to be with Jonah in a way I've never needed anything. He is my protector, my shield.

I strip out of my clothes. No shame, no worry, no fear.

In Jonah's presence, I am safe. Here, I am home.

## Chapter Nineteen

# JONAH

She stands before me naked, her heart and soul bared to me. She remembers. She fucking remembers.

This was my deepest wish, my never-ending prayer.

Her body is so beautiful, a scar across her tummy, signaling her strength. She carried our daughter against all odds, she gave her life and now she stands here before me, so damn strong.

"I love you, Faith," I say, my hand tangled in her hair, my mouth crashing against her lips. "I love you, I love you, I love you," I whisper over and over. Words I've wanted to say to her day and night, words I wanted her to hear, words she can now accept because she knows my love is real, forever.

A towel is the only thing I wear, and I wrap her in my arms, her cheek against my chest, my heart beating against her ear. My cock lengthens as I hold the love of my life against me.

She tugs on the towel, it falls to the floor. She whimpers at the sight of me, her hand running over my shaft. "I remember," she moans. "God, Jonah, I miss you."

I run my hands gently over her breasts, they are tender and full, and she closes her eyes as I caress her. "You are so perfect," I tell her. Every inch of her body is so enticing, every part of her skin begging to be licked, touched, explored.

"You're so hard... so big," she breathes, her fingers on my balls, my growing cock, she licks her lips. She is hungry too.

"Are you ready?" I ask. Ocean was born only a little over six weeks ago.

She nods. "The doctor cleared me, but we need to go slow," she says.

I cup her face with my hands, our eyes meeting, glassy and full of promise. "We have all the time in the world, Faith."

She smiles, a tear on her cheek. "We have a baby, Jonah. We are a family," she says, the reality just sinking in.

"We are." I smile, pulling her lips to mine. Kissing her softly. "And Faith, you were so beautiful pregnant. Your belly was huge, and I would sit with you, feeling our baby kick, imagining this moment. All of us here, whole, healthy. One."

"My body looks so different now," she says. "I have more curves, that's for sure."

"I love them," I tell her. Her cheeks are pink, and I'm guessing she is both excited and nervous. It's been so long.

"You are so good to me, Jonah. You never gave up."

"I had faith in us."

She wraps her arms around me. "Make love to me, please."

I will never make her wait. We move to the bed,

and I lay her down, on the edge. I spread her knees, kneeling before her. Kissing her thighs, her creamy skin. Kissing her gently, with care.

"Please," she moans, and I pull her hips to the edge of the bed, standing before her, easing my cock inside nice and slow. I lift her legs, and she hooks them over my shoulders. It's easier on her still-healing scar this way. Her tits are so big and round, and they bounce as I begin to fill her warm and ready cunt. She is eager and slick, and she needs this. Me.

"Oh, Jonah," she purrs, her fingers gripping the blankets on the bed. "Oh baby," she whimpers as I move in a rhythm that is made for her alone.

"You like that, golden girl?"

She moans in delight. "I love it."

I fill her tight pussy up, the way she begs. My cock throbs as it moves against her pulsing need. "You feel so good, Faith," I moan, my release coming to a head as I fuck her, my hands running over her bare legs, loving the way it feels to be so close to her. Connected. Finally.

She is so close to the edge, she has been waiting for this moment as long as I have, needy and desperate to be back here, in this bed, making love.

"Oh, Jonah," she whimpers as my come fills her tight little channel, her own orgasm building, and washing over her as my hot seed warms her cunt. She is gasping, panting as we finish, her body trembling with pleasure as I pull my still thick cock from her.

I lie beside her in the bed, pulling her close. "You okay?"

She smiles, serenity written on her face. "More than."

I reach into the drawer of my bedside table and pull out the one thing I have been waiting to offer her.

"Faith," I say, running my fingers over her arm, gratitude swelling within me.

"What is it?" she asks softly.

"I asked you this once before, and you said yes, but now I am asking you again — this time with a different understanding of the word love; a more complete definition of the word commitment sealed on my heart. Faith, will you marry me?"

Her eyes glisten, golden flecks dancing against the dark green. "Yes, Jonah, I will marry you."

I offer her the ring, a rose gold diamond set on a gold band. "For my golden girl," I say, sliding it on her delicate finger. It's shiny and bright, just like her.

"It's perfect," she says, burying her face in my chest. "We are so lucky, Jonah, so lucky."

I kiss her again, anxious to marry the woman I love. This time I already have her father's approval, this time there will be no running away in cars. This time there will only be slow kisses and the steady beat of our hearts. We don't need to rush into this — we know now that it isn't the destination, it's the journey.

I purchased the ring weeks after she entered the coma, knowing there were no guarantees, but I didn't need guarantees.

All I needed was Faith.

# EPILOGUE 1

## Faith

### NINE MONTHS LATER...

The lake is calm, the sun glitters off the waves. As I walk down the aisle with my dad holding my arm, my heart beats hard. I am alive, I am here, breathing, strong, surrounded by everyone I love.

Our friends sit in white chairs, facing the lake, and I walk past them all, telling myself to keep it together — but it's no use. Tears streak my cheeks as I take the beauty that surrounds me.

I see Harper sitting with her children, Cedar, Alder, and Spruce, and a daughter Violet, who is one year younger, and another year younger, her brother Riggs.

Buck and Rosie sit in another row, with their twins Clover and Poppy and their younger daughter Lola.

Wilder and Stella are here with their older twins Briar and Finn, and the younger set of twins Boomer and Brantley. Stella's eyes meet mine and I feel her love for our family — everyone's love, really.

Honor and Hawk sit opposite them holding hands, with their sons Timothy, Thomas and Titus and twin girls Ettie and Imogen.

James has his arms around his wife Cherish. Sitting next to them is their older set of triplets, Jamie, their daughter, and Jacob and Andrew. And their second set of triplets, just a year younger, are two girls named Magnolia and Maybelline, and one boy, Oakley.

Beau and Josie sit with their son Forrest and their twin daughters Hattie and Hazel. Josie can't stop crying, and I feel a new wave of gratitude sweeping over me. Jonah and I have so much support with us here today.

Grace and Bear are here, too, with their twins

Laura and Abel, and their triplets, two boys—Canyon and Ridge, and a daughter, Greta.

Colton and Laila are here with their quadruplets, Beatrix, Dorothy, Asher, and Bennett.

And Virginia, my step-mom, is in the front row with her youngest daughter Daisy in a sling, and Ava, sitting on my sister Willa's lap. Beside them sits Levi, Lily, Clover, and Cash.

And at the end of the aisle stands Jonah, holding Ocean in his arms. She claps, so happy to see me. Her mama. The lake is behind them, flowers are wrapped around the arbor that surrounds us. The ceremony is beautiful — so many hands went into helping make this a perfect day — but the really beautiful thing is that we are all here together, everyone who makes Miracle Mountain such a special place has joined us here to watch Jonah and I commit to one another until death do us part.

"Oh, Daddy," I say, squeezing my dad's arm as he pulls me into a hug before giving me away. "I love you."

"I'm so proud of you, Faith," he tells me. And I

know he is. I know this whole mountain is proud of Jonah and me.

Jaxon marries us, and Dad sits on a stool, playing the guitar and singing us a song he wrote for this day. It's become a hit, having released two weeks ago. It's been a Billboard top ten song. Every time our daughter hears it play, she starts bouncing up and down.

*"I have faith that love will see us through, I have faith in me and you.*

*I have faith as deep as the ocean, as wide as a whale.*

*I have faith in our forever, and I know that time does heal."*

At the end of the ceremony, Jonah pulls me into his arms as Jaxon tells him to kiss his bride.

His lips are soft, firm. Our kiss is the start of another chapter in our story. A story that is turning into a series. And, gosh, when I look around the families gathered here for our wedding, I am reminded how our lives have woven together in so many ways. We've overcome obstacles — every single couple here. Fought for the love that we've found. We know they value family because it is family time and time again that has seen us through.

Everyone stands, cheering for us as we head to the tent where a dance floor is waiting, where a BBQ feast is all prepared — potato salad and corn on the cob, grilled meat, and watermelon. This mountain was built on more than love — potlucks are the backbone, and so our reception reflects that. Everyone pitched in, not because we couldn't afford a caterer, but because the symbolism is what I want to carry into my marriage. That none of us can do it alone, and we don't have to. Not when there is a mountain of people ready to pitch in and lend a helping hand.

There was a time where I couldn't remember the most important person in my life. So now, I spend extra time memorizing everything.

These moments, the smiles, the laughter, the children running in circles, blowing bubbles. The friends and family gathered around Jonah and me as we celebrate. I close my eyes and hold these moments tight. I'll never let them go.

Jonah and I cut our wedding cake. Josie made it for us as our gift. White buttercream frosting that gets all over Jonah's face as I smash it against his mouth, pulling my husband in for a sugary sweet kiss. Later, I will pull him in for so much more.

Music plays for hours, lights are strung through all the trees. Dad has Ocean in his arms. Jonah pulls me in close as we slow dance. I blink back tears at the miracle that we have found in one another.

At the miracle that is our love story.

# EPILOGUE 2

## Jonah

### TEN YEARS LATER...

I'm in my office, working on my novel, when Faith walks in, carrying a tray with my lunch.

"This is a surprise," I say, grinning at my gorgeous wife.

"I needed a break. Am I interrupting?"

I push away from the desk, watching as Faith bends over to set the tray on the coffee table. Damn, she looks so fucking hot today. Every day. Ten years later and I know I am the luckiest man on this goddamn mountain — she is my dream come true.

"Not interrupting anything." I reach for her

waist, turning her toward me. "You have writer's block too?"

She groans, looking up into my eyes. "So badly. And my editor is waiting for the draft, but I just feel all anxious about it."

I tuck a strand of hair behind her ear. "You know, I could help clear your head."

She licks her lips. "Is that so?"

I grin, squeezing her round ass. "Yes, I can."

She lets her head fall back. "I need to get Ocean and Emerson from school in an hour. And that's when you need to leave. Cedar is expecting you to meet him at Rosie's diner to go over his college application."

I run my hand under her dress, a short skirt with nothing but a tiny pair of panties underneath. Perfect. "So, you're saying we have plenty of time?"

She laughs, her laugh as airy and breathless as it ever was. Even after all this time — a decade — she is still the same girl I met all those years ago. Now we have a son, too; two years younger than Ocean. Faith has released two bestselling novels, I have published three books, including my memoir— which was a runaway bestseller. We tore down our cabin years ago and built a gorgeous lakefront home.

The guys on the mountain joke that I've turned this place into my little version of Walden, a lakeside oasis. But I'm still as much a mountain man as ever — I chop our wood in the winter, have calluses on my hand to prove I know the meaning of hard work and true grit. If someone needs help putting up a house, cabin, or most often, a swing set for their kids, I am always the first to pitch in and help.

But I have a reason to stay home as much as possible. It starts and ends with Faith — my homebody of a wife who makes it hella hard to get out of bed most mornings.

Now, Faith unbuckles my jeans, and I groan as she takes ahold of my firm, stiff cock. "Oh, golden girl." I run my hand over her back, unhooking her bra. Needing her big round tits in my palm, my other hand easing down her panties, needing to touch her slick cunt. Getting her nice and ready for my thickness.

"That feels so good," she tells me as I press a finger in her tight little pussy, then another.

She's is already so sweet and creamy as I begin to finger her. I smile. "Someone was horny."

"I was," she laughs softly, biting my shoulder. "God, Jonah, I was upstairs in my office, staring at the computer and all I could think about was you making me come." She unbuttons my flannel, and I toss it aside. Her fingers run over my biceps, the tattoo that I got after Ocean was born, a whale tattoo for her, for our daughter, and later another one for Emerson.

"That's fucking hot," I tell her, loving that she was thinking about getting fucked by her one true love.

"Oh, Jonah," she whimpers, as I stroke her faster, then she's dropping to her knees, taking me in her mouth. Her lips wrap around my hard cock and she begins to suck my length, taking me deeper and deeper, looking up in my eyes as she gets me off.

"Fuck," I groan, my cock throbbing as she swirls her tongue over my hard ridges. And I know she's gonna make me come nice and hard, and soon.

"Come here, Goldie," I tell her, easing her back up to stand, pushing aside the papers and folders on my desk, needing to fuck my wife hard and dirty.

She sits on my desk, her dripping cunt my goddamn prize, and I fill her up in one swift movement, and she gasps, the fullness of me inside her taking her breath away.

Her tits bounce as I take her, her skin soft as I run my hands over her, memorizing this — all of it — like I always do. I take nothing for granted, time is precious, every minute, every hour, every day.

"Oh, Jonah," she moans. "I'm so close. My pussy is so... so... oh, god," she moans, her arms around my neck as I thrust myself against her heat.

"I love you," I tell her as my thick cock releases deep inside her. "I love you so damn much."

She gasps for breath, her hands on my chest as the orgasm rolls over her. "Good," she says. "Because..."

"Because what?" I ask. The look in her eyes is one I don't see very often. Like she has been keeping something from me.

"Because we're having another baby."

My eyes widen, and I pick my wife up off the desk and her legs wrap around me. "Seriously?"

She laughs. "Are you shocked?"

"I'm fucking thrilled."

"I just took the test, that's why I couldn't focus... and then I took it and I was thinking about you, and how you're the hottest baby daddy ever and... well," she laughs. "It got me all worked up."

I press my forehead to hers. "God, this is everything, Faith."

"It is, isn't it?" Her smile is contagious, my grin is so broad. My heart so fucking full.

I keep her in my lap, sitting down on the couch in my office. I lace my fingers with hers, knowing how much she has been wanting to get pregnant. We tried for several years after Emerson, even did two rounds of IVF. It seemed like its wasn't meant to be. And we felt that we had more than enough blessings with our two amazing children.

"What are you thinking?" she asks me, my thoughts tracing over our history, our story.

"It's another miracle, isn't it?" I say.

She nods, tears in her eyes. "Miracles are always waiting for the open-hearted."

I kiss her, holding her in my arms. Soft and slow. Choosing to believe that we have forever. And in this moment, time seems to still. I hold my wife, her lips on mine, knowing that we haven't even seen half of it yet — life has so many more miracles to offer.

And I have faith that love will always see us through.

---

# PREVIEW

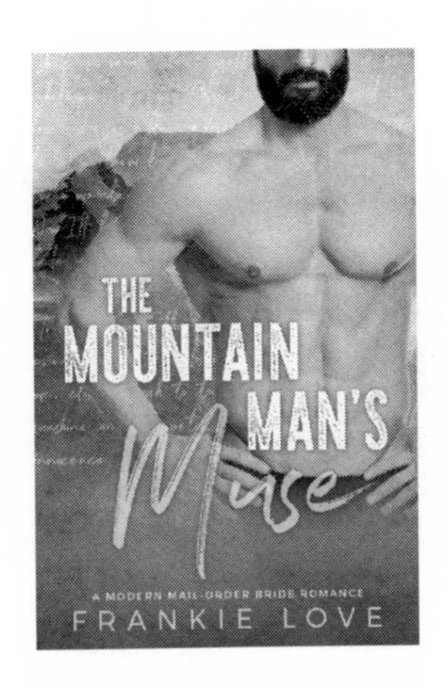


When River orders a wife, he's hoping she'll cure his writer's block.
But when he meets his bride, he knows she's more than a quick-fix— she's his muse.

Rose needs a quiet place to record her yoga videos, and a lakeside cabin in the middle of nowhere is better than her L.A. apartment.
Yes, it means she's a mail-order bride, but Rose isn't scared of a challenge.
River is handsome and knows how to use his hands. So what if he's a bit of a recluse?
She'll take a deep breath and take it one day at a time.
Except someone is after her— and tracking her every move.
She may be his muse—but she needs a hero.

*Dear Reader,*
*River's more than a mountain man; he's a romantic at heart.*
*He'll make you swoon, sweat, and have you packing your bags to be the next mail-order bride in this series.*
*xo, frankie*

Download here (click title)
The Mountain Man's Muse

## ABOUT THE AUTHOR

**Frankie Love** writes filthy-sweet stories about bad boys and mountain men. As a thirty-something mom who is ridiculously in love with her own bearded hottie, she believes in love-at-first-sight and happily-ever-afters.

She also believes in the power of a quickie.

*Find Frankie here:*
www.frankielove.net